CHRISTMAS
IN MY HEART® 28

CHRISTMAS IN MY HEART 28 ®

THE BEST OF BOOKS 1–13

JOE L. WHEELER

Pacific Press®
Publishing Association

Nampa, Idaho | www.pacificpress.com

Cover design by Steve Lanto
Cover design resources from iStockphoto.com | 154308981

The author assumes full responsibility for the accuracy of all facts and quotations as cited in this book.

Additional copies of this book are available by calling toll-free 1-800-765-6955 or by visiting www.AdventistBookCenter.com.

Library of Congress Cataloging-in-Publication Data

Names: Wheeler, Joe L., 1936- compiler, editor.
Title: Christmas in my heart : a treasury of old-fashioned Christmas stories / compiled and edited by Joe L. Wheeler.
Other titles: Christmas in my heart. Selections.
Description: Nampa, Idaho : Pacific Press Publishing Association, 2019. | Series: Christmas in my heart; 28 | "The best of books 1-13." | Includes bibliographical references. | Summary: "This collection of classic Christmas stories, part of the longest-running Christmas story series in America, contains the author's favorite entries from books one through thirteen"—Provided by publisher.
Identifiers: LCCN 2019029039 | ISBN 9780816362691 (paperback)
Subjects: LCSH: Christmas stories, American.
Classification: LCC PS648.C45 C4472 2019 | DDC 813/.0108334—dc23
LC record available at https://lccn.loc.gov/2019029039

July 2019

Dedication

In this strange journey called "life," so many people interact with us that it is often difficult to know which ones made the greatest difference in our lives and achievements. And sometimes we wait too long to express that appreciation. Sadly, this is true today as I write this dedication.

I first knew him as one of our most talented college students; then, many years later, on an entirely different level, he came back into my life. This time, *he* was to call the shots, not me. Through the years, I have worked with many editors, but none of them stand out in memory more than this year's honoree. No matter how busy he may have been, somehow he always found time to quickly respond to all of my questions—and they were *many!* Often, even when he was on the road, he'd email me the moment he heard from me. So many of our 102 books bear the imprint of his mind and heart. Invariably, he was kind. And his laughs were invariably day-brighteners. And so, belatedly (he recently passed away), I am today dedicating *Christmas in My Heart*® *28* to my student, my long-time editor, my cherished friend, and the former editorial vice president at Pacific Press Publishing Association.

JERRY D. THOMAS
(10/30/1959–3/15/2019)

Books by Joe L. Wheeler

Acknowledgments

" 'Meditation' in a Minor Key," by Joseph Leininger Wheeler. Written in 1991; revised in 1992. Printed by permission of the author.

"The Littlest Orphan and the Christ Baby," by Margaret E. Sangster. Featured in Sangster's collection *The Littlest Orphan and Other Christmas Stories* (New York: Round Table Press, 1918). If anyone can provide knowledge of the first publication source of this old story, please relay information to Joe L. Wheeler, care of Pacific Press®, Nampa, Idaho.

"Rebecca's Only Way," by Annie Hamilton Donnell. Published in *The Youth's Instructor*, December 18, 1928. Reprinted by permission of the Review and Herald® Publishing Association.

"Pink Angel," author unknown. If anyone can provide knowledge of authorship, origin, and first publication source of this old story, please relay this information to Joe L. Wheeler, care of Pacific Press®, Nampa, Idaho.

"Christmas in Tin Can Valley," author unknown. If anyone can provide knowledge of authorship, origin, and first publication source of this old story, please relay this information to Joe L. Wheeler, care of Pacific Press®, Nampa, Idaho.

"A Stolen Christmas," by Charles M. Sheldon. Reprinted by permission of Christian Herald Association.

"His Last Christmas," by Joseph Leininger Wheeler. Copyright 1998. Reprinted by permission of the author.

"Legacy," by Joseph Leininger Wheeler. Copyright 1999. Reprinted by permission of the author.

"An Ill Wind," by Frederick William Roe. Published in *The Youth's Companion*, January 2, 1919. Reprinted by permission of David C. Cook Publishing, Colorado Springs, Colorado.

"Johnny Christmas," author unknown. If anyone can provide knowledge of authorship, origin, and first publication source of this old story, please relay this information to Joe L. Wheeler, care of Pacific Press®, Nampa, Idaho.

"At Lowest Ebb," author unknown. If anyone can provide knowledge of authorship, origin, and first publication source of this old story, please relay this information to Joe L. Wheeler, care of Pacific Press®, Nampa, Idaho.

"Van Valkenberg's Christmas Gift," by Elizabeth G. Jordan. If anyone can provide knowledge of the first publication source of this story, please relay this information to Joe L. Wheeler, care of Pacific Press®, Nampa, Idaho.

"A White Christmas," author unknown. If anyone can provide knowledge of authorship, origin, and first publication source of this old story, please relay this information to Joe L. Wheeler, care of Pacific Press®, Nampa, Idaho.

Contents

DECEM-
BER

MERRIE
X☓MAS

Preface

Christmas in My Heart® and Joe Wheeler are inextricably connected in a beautiful reminder of the message of the season. The power in these stories over the last twenty-seven years transcend the elegant writing and the delicate narratives; it pulsates with the hope of the greatest story from the heart of a profoundly spiritual writer and compiler.

In a world shaken by doubt, cynicism and superficial pursuits, the Christmas in My Heart® collection speaks of the natural yearning of the human heart for the love we glimpse in the face of Bethlehem's Baby. If nostalgia for simpler times has made it the "longest-running Christmas story series in America;" there is inherent goodness in the values of generosity, kindness, courage, and gratitude found in its pages.

The volume you hold in your hand is a celebration of the first thirteen years of this collection, with a story from each of those books. Although many have collected the whole series over the years, this year's compilation offers a taste of the early years of the collection for those who haven't. The next volume will include stories from the last fourteen years of Christmas in My Heart®. We hope there will be other volumes in this collection; for now, we are tremendously grateful to Joe Wheeler for making Christmas in My Heart® such an uplifting Christmas tradition.

Pacific Press Editors
July 2019

"Meditation" in a Minor Key

by Joseph Leininger Wheeler

Twenty-seven years ago (in 1992), our first collection of Christmas stories (Christmas in My Heart) rolled off the presses of Review and Herald® Publishing Association in Hagerstown, Maryland. Back then, we had not even an inkling that the modest little 128-page book would end up changing our lives. Nor did we even dream that it would touch so many hearts that it would eventually become the longest-running Christmas story series in America. Neither our publisher nor we had any idea as to what we had just given birth to or that it would live longer than twelve months. No number "1" appeared on the cover to even hint to readers that someday there might possibly be a sequel.

We thought it was good—how good we should have known when our book editor, Penny Estes Wheeler [no relation], prefaced her first phone call to me with these words: "Joe, the committee has cried its way through your manuscript."

The book's success was foreordained by my mother's love of story, readings, and poetry. An elocutionist of the old school, even when still in high school, Mother could hold audiences in the palm of her hand; at the end, she'd wring them out to dry. I've long felt God preordained me to carry on the story torch after her storytelling days were over.

We have been humbled and often overwhelmed by torrents of unsolicited letters of appreciation for caring enough to create a new Christmas story collection every year. We've never felt personal ownership of the series: from the beginning to this day it has been a God thing—never a Wheeler thing. How amazing that our Lord condescends to partner with the least of His children.

Not long before we sent in our manuscript for our first book, I was convicted that I ought to write a Christmas story of my own. The catalyst was a piece of music I had long loved. As far as I knew, it had no Christmas roots or tie-ins whatsoever. All I knew was that it was so hauntingly beautiful that I could not even listen to it without weeping. It was Massenet's "Meditation," often publicly performed on a violin.

As I wrote my rough draft, I constantly prayed that God would cowrite it with me. Later, Virginia Fagel, a professional violinist and cherished friend, wrote me a letter in which were these words: "Joe, I just finished reading your new story, ' "Meditation" in a Minor Key.' That was such a wonderful story that you and God wrote."

Another serendipity was that Ingrid Vargas, a double major of English and music at Washington Adventist University, asked if she might read the story as it was being written. Since she is a perfectionist, she insisted that every sentence, every paragraph in the story be perfect. She'd even call me up in the middle of the night, grousing that certain lines were not quite perfect. Thanks to divine inspiration and Ms. Vargas's dedicated proofreading, the story approaches the sublime. I have received more mail responses to this story than any other story I have ever written. And thanks to these responses, I have written a new Christmas story for each Christmas collection since then.

I later discovered that "Meditation" was written by Massenet as a musical bridge between the secular and spiritual realms of our lives—hence its emotive power.

* * * * *

"Eight minutes until curtain time, Mr. Devereaux."

"How's it looking?"

"Full house. No. *More* than full house—they're already turning away those who'll accept Standing Room Only tickets."

"Frankly, I'm a bit surprised, Mr. Schobel. My last concert here was not much of a success."

"I remember, sir. . . . The house was barely a third full."

"Hmm. I wonder . . . uh . . . what do you suppose has made the difference?"

"Well, for one thing, sir, it's your first-ever Christmas concert. For another, people are regaining interest—that Deutsche Gramophone recording has all Europe talking. But pardon me, sir. I'd better let you get ready. Good luck, sir."

And he was gone.

* * * * *

No question about it, he mused as he bowed to acknowledge the applause, the venerable opera house was indeed full. As always, his eyes panned the sea of faces as he vainly searched for the one who never came—had not in ten long years. He had *so* hoped tonight would be different.

That package—it hadn't done the job after all. . . .

Ten years ago . . . tonight . . . it was. Right here in Old Vienna. It was to have been the happiest Christmas Eve in his life: was not Ginevra to become his bride the next day?

What a fairy-tale courtship that had been. It had all started at the Salzburg Music Festival, where he was the center of attention—not only of the city but of the world. Had he not stunned concert-goers by his incredible coup? The first pianist to ever win grand piano's Triple Crown: the Van Cliburn, the Queen Elizabeth, and the Tchaikovsky competitions?

Fame had built steadily for him as one after another of the great prizes had fallen to him. Now, as reporters, interviewers, and cameramen followed his every move, he grew drunk on the wine of adulation.

It happened as he leaned over the parapet of Salzburg Castle, watching the morning sun gild the rooftops of the city below. He had risen early in order to hike up the hill to the castle and watch the sunrise. A cool alpine breeze ruffled the trees just above—but it also displaced a few strands of raven black hair only a few feet to his left. Their glances met—and they both glanced away, only to blush as they glanced back. She was the most beautiful girl he had ever seen. But beautiful in more than mere appearance: beautiful in poise and grace as well. Later, he would gradually discover her beauty of soul.

With uncharacteristic shyness, he introduced himself to her. And then she withdrew in confusion as she tied the name to the cover stories. Disarming her with a smile, he quickly changed the subject: What was *she* doing in Salzburg?

As it turned out, she was in Europe for a summer-long study tour—and how his heart leaped when she admitted that her study group was staying in Salzburg the entire week. He made the most of it: before her bus had moved on he had pried from her not very reluctant fingers a copy of the tour itinerary.

And like Jean Valjean's inexorable nemesis, Javert, he pursued her all over Europe, driving his concert manager into towering rages. Had he forgotten that there was the long and arduous fall schedule to prepare for? Had he forgotten the time it took to memorize a new repertoire? No, he hadn't forgotten. The truth of the matter was that his priorities had suddenly changed. Every midweek, in around-the-clock marathons, he'd give his practicing its due—then he'd escape in order to be with Ginevra for the weekend.

They were instant soul mates. They both loved the mountains and the sea, dawn and dusk, Tolstoy and Twain, snow and sand, hiking and skiing, Gothic cathedrals and medieval castles, sidewalk cafes and old bookstores. But they were not clones: in art, she loved Georges de la Tour and Caravaggio whereas his patron saints were Dürer and Hieronymus Bosch; in music, he preferred Mozart and Prokofiev whereas she reveled in Chopin and Liszt.

He knew the day he met her that, for him, there would never be another woman. He was that rarity: a man who out of the whole world will choose but one—and if that one be denied him. . . .

But he wasn't denied. It was on the last day of her stay, just hours before she boarded her plane for home, that he asked her to climb with him the zig-zagging inner staircases of the bell tower of Votivkirche, that great neo-Gothic cathedral of Vienna, paling in comparison only with its legendary ancestor, Saint Stephen's.

Far up in the tower, breathing hard for more than one reason, his voice shook as he took both her hands captive . . . and looked through her honest eyes into her heart—his, he knew, even without asking. She never *did* actually say yes, for the adorable curl of her lips, coupled with the candle-lit road to heaven in her eyes, was her undoing.

The rapture which followed comes only once in a lifetime—when it comes at all.

Then the scene changed, and he stiffened as if receiving a mortal blow, for but four months later, in that self-same bell tower, his world had come to an end. That terrible, terrible night when his nuptial dreams were slain by a violin.

* * * * *

Ginevra drew her heavy coat tighter around her as the airport limousine disappeared into the night. Inside the opera house she made her way to the ticket counter to ask for directions to her section.

From the other side of the doors she heard Bach's "Italian Concerto" being reborn. . . . She listened intently. She had not been mistaken after all: a change *had* taken place.

Leaning against a pillar, she let the distant notes wash over her while she took the scroll of her life and unrolled a third of it. How vividly she remembered that memorable fall. Michael's letters came as regularly as night following

day: long letters most of the time, short messages when his hectic schedule precluded more. Her pattern was unvarying: she would walk up the mountain road to the mailbox, out of the day's mail search for that precious envelope, then carry it unopened on top of the rest of the mail back to the chalet, perched high on a promontory point 1,600 feet above the Denver plain. Then she'd walk out onto the upper deck and seat herself. Off to her right were the Flat-irons massed above the city of Boulder. Front and center below was the skyline of Denver—at night a fairyland of twinkling lights; to the left, the mountains stair-stepped up to 14,259-foot Longs Peak and Rocky Mountain National Park. Then she'd listen for the pines—oh! those heav-enly pines! They would be sighing their haunting song . . . and *then* she would open his letter.

So full of romance were her starlit eyes that weeks passed before she realized there was a hairline crack in her heart—and Michael was the cause of it. She hadn't realized it during that idyllic summer as the two of them had spent so much time exploring Gothic cathedrals, gazing trans-fixed as light transformed stained-glass into heart-stopping glory, sitting on transepts as organists opened their stops and called on their pipes to dare the red zone of reverber-ating sound.

She finally, in a long letter, asked him point-blank whether or not he believed in God. His response was a masterpiece of subterfuge and fence-straddling, for well he knew how central the Lord was to her. As women have ever since the dawn of time, she rationalized that if he just loved *her* enough—and surely he *did*—then of course he would come to love God as much as she.

So it was that she put her reservations and premonitions aside and deflected her parents' concerns in that respect as well. Michael had decided he wanted to be married in the same cathedral where he had proposed to her, and, as it was large enough to accommodate family as well as key figures of the music world, she had reluctantly acquiesced. Personally, she would have much rather been married in the small Boulder church high up on Mapleton Avenue. A Christmas wedding there, in the church she so loved . . . but it was not to be.

Deciding to make the best of it, she and her family drove down the mountain, took the freeway to Stapleton Airport, boarded the plane, and found their seats. As the big United jet roared off the runway, she looked out the window at Denver and her beloved Colorado receding below her. She wondered: could Michael's European world ever really take its place?

It was cold that memorable Christmas Eve, and the snow lay several feet deep on Viennese streets. Ginevra, ever the romantic, shyly asked Michael if he would make a special pilgrimage with her.

"Where to?" queried Michael. "It's mighty cold out-side."

"The bell tower of Votivkirche."

He grinned that boyish grin she loved. "I really *am* mar-rying a sentimentalist, aren't I? Oh well," he complained good-naturedly, "guess I'd better get used to it. Let's find our coats."

An unearthly quiet came over the great city as they once again climbed the winding staircases of Votivkirche. She caught her breath at the beauty of it all when they

at last reached their eyrie and looked down at the frosted rooftops and streets below. Michael, however, much preferred the vision *she* represented in her flame-colored dress and sable coat.

Then it was . . . faintly and far away . . . that they heard it. They never did trace its origin exactly. It might have wafted its way up the tower from below, or it might have come from an apartment across the way. Ordinarily, in the cacophony of the city, they could not possibly have heard it, but tonight, with snow deadening the street sounds, they could distinctly pick up every note. Whoever the violinist was . . . was a master.

Ginevra listened: transfixed. Michael, noting her tear-stained cheeks, shattered the moment with an ill-timed laugh. "Why you old crybaby, it's nothing but a song! I've heard it somewhere before. I don't remember who wrote it, but it's certainly nothing to cry over."

He checked as he saw her recoil as if he had slashed her face with a whip. Her face blanched, and she struggled for control. After a long pause, she said in a toneless voice: "It's not a song—it's 'Meditation' by Massenet."

"Well, that's fine with me," quipped Michael; "I'll just meditate about *you*."

There was a long silence, and now, quite ill at ease, he shuffled his feet and tried to pass it all off as a joke.

But in that, he failed abysmally: "You . . . you don't hear it at all," she cried. "You just don't. . . . I never hear that melody without tears, or without soaring to heaven on the notes. Massenet *had* to have been a Christian! And, furthermore, whoever plays it like we just heard it played *has* to be a Christian too!"

"Oh, come now, Ginevra. Aren't you getting carried away by a simple little ditty? *Anyone* who really knows how to play the violin could play it just as well. . . . I certainly could—and I don't even believe in . . . in God—" He stopped, vainly trying to slam his lips on the words in time, but perversely they slipped out of their own accord.

Deep within the citadel of her innermost being, Ginevra felt her heart shudder as if seized by two powerful opposing forces. Then—where the hairline crack of her heart once was—there was an awful *crack*—and a yawning fault took its place.

The look of agony on her face brought him to his senses at last—but it was too late. She looked at him with glaciered cheeks and with eyes so frozen that he could barely discern the tiny flickering that had, only moments ago, almost overpowered him with the glow of a thousand lovelit candles.

She turned, slipped something which had once been on her finger into his coat pocket, and was gone. So quickly was the act done that at first he failed to realize she was no longer there. Then he called after her and ran blindly down the stairs. Ginevra, however, with the instinct of a wounded animal, found an unlocked stairwell door and hid inside until he had raced down the tower and into the street. Much later, she silently made her way out into a world made glad by midnight bells. But there was no Christmas gladness in *her* heart.

She determined to never see him again. Neither his calls nor his letters nor his telegrams would she answer; writing him only once: "Please do not *ever* try to contact me in any way again."

And he—his pride in shreds—never had.

* * * * *

Never would he forget that awful Christmas when—*alone*—he had to face the several thousand wedding guests and the importunate press with the news that it was all off. No, he could give them no reasons. And then he had fled.

Since he had planned on an extended honeymoon, he had no more concerts scheduled until the next fall. That winter and spring he spent much time in solitude, moping and feeling sorry for himself. By late spring, he was stir-crazy, so he fled to the South Pacific, to Asia, to Africa, to South America—*anywhere* to get away from himself and his memories.

Somehow, by midsummer, he began to regain control; he returned to Europe and quickly mastered his fall repertoire. That fall, most of his reviews were of the rave variety, for he dazzled with his virtuosity and technique.

For several years, his successes continued, and audiences filled concert halls wherever he performed. But there came a day when that was no longer true, when he realized that most dreaded of performing world truths: that it was all over—he had peaked. Here he was, his career hardly begun, and his star was already setting. But *why*?

Reviewers and concert-goers alike tried vainly to diagnose the ailment and prescribe medicinal cures, but nothing worked. More and more the tenor of the reviews began to sound like the following:

"How sad it is that Devereaux—once thought to be the rising star of our age: the worthy successor to Horowitz—has been revealed as but human clay after all. It is as if he represents but a case of arrested development. Normally, as a pianist lives and ages, the roots sink deeper and the storm-battered trunk and branches develop seasoning and rugged strength. Not so with Devereaux. It's as if all growth ceased some time ago. Oh! No one can match him where it comes to razzle-dazzle and special effects, but one gets a bit tired of these when there is no offsetting depth."

Like a baseball slugger in a prolonged batting slump, Michael tried everything: he dabbled in every philosophy or mysticism he came across. Like a drunken bee, he reeled from flower to flower without any real sense of direction.

And "Meditation" had gradually become an obsession with him. He just couldn't seem to get it out of his consciousness. He determined to prove to her that you didn't have to be religious in order to play it well. But as much as he tried, as much as he applied his vaunted techniques and interpretive virtuosity to it, it yet remained as flat, stale, and unmoving as three-hour-old coffee.

He even went to the trouble of researching the tune's origins, feeling confident that it, like much music concert performers play, would apparently have no religious connections whatsoever. In his research, he discovered that "Meditation" came from Massenet's opera *Thaïs*, which he knew had to do with a dissolute courtesan. Aha! He had her! But then, he dug deeper and discovered, to his chagrin, that although it was true that *Thaïs* had a dissolute sexual past, as was true with Mary Magdalene, she was redeemed—and "Meditation" represents the intermezzo bridge between the pagan past of the first two acts and the oneness with God in the third act.

So he had to acknowledge defeat here too.

As for Ginevra, she was never far from his thoughts. But not once would his pride permit him to ask anyone about her, her career, or whether or not she had ever married.

He just *existed* . . . and measured his life by concerts and hotel rooms.

* * * * *

Ginevra too, after the long numbness and shock had at last weathered into a reluctant peace, belatedly realized that life had to go on . . . but just what should she do with her life?

It was during a freak spring blizzard that snowed her in that the answer came. She had been sitting in the conversation pit of the three-story-high massive moss rock fireplace, gazing dreamily into the fire, when suddenly, the mood came upon her to write. She reached for a piece of paper, picked up her Pilot pen, and began writing a poem. A poem about pain, disillusion, and heartbreak. The next day, she mailed it off to a magazine. Not long after, it was published.

She decided to do graduate work in the humanities and in education. She completed, along the way, a master's, and later a PhD; in the process, becoming the world's foremost authority on the life and times of a woman writer of the American heartland. She also continued, as her busy schedule permitted, to write poems, essays, short stories, inspirational literature, and longer works of fiction.

So it was that Ginevra became a teacher: a teacher of writing, of literature—and life. Each class was a microcosm of life itself; in each class were souls crying out to be ministered to, to be appreciated, to be loved.

Because of her charm, vivacity, *joie du vivre*, and sense of humor, she became ever more popular and beloved with the passing of the years. She attracted suitors like children to a toy store. Yet, though some of these friendships got to the threshold of love, none of them got any further: it was as if not one of them could match what she had left behind in Vienna.

The good Lord it was who saw her through: who shored up her frailties and helped to mend the brokenness.

Meanwhile, she did find time to keep up with Michael's life and career. In doing so, she bought all his recordings, and played them often. Yet, she was vaguely dissatisfied: she too noting the lack of growth—and wondered.

One balmy day in late November during the seventh year after the breakup, as she was walking down the ridge to her home, she stopped to listen to her two favorite sounds: the cascading creek cavorting its way down to the Front Range plain and the sibilant whispering of the pines. Leaning against a large rock, she looked up at that incredibly blue sky of the Colorado high country.

As always, her thoughts refused to stay in their neat little cages. She had tried all kinds of locks during those seven years, but not one of them worked. And now, when she had thought them safely locked in, here came all her truant thoughts: bounding up to her like a rag-tag litter of exuberant puppies, overjoyed at finding her hiding place.

And every last one of the little mutts was yelping Michael's name.

What would *he* be doing this Christmas. It bothered

her—had bothered her for almost seven years now—that her own judge had refused to acquit her for her Michael-related words and actions. Periodically, during these years, she had submitted her case to the judge in the courthouse of her mind; and every last time, after listening to the evidence, the judge had looked at her stern-faced. She would bang the gavel on the judicial bench and intone severely: "Insufficient evidence on which to absolve you. . . . Next case?"

She couldn't get out of her head an article she had read several months before—an article about Michael Devereaux. The writer, who had interviewed her subject in depth, had done her homework well: for the portrait of Michael rang true to Ginevra. The individual revealed in the character sketch was both the Michael whom Ginevra knew and a Michael she would rather not know. The interviewer pointed out that Michael was a rather bitter man for one so young in years. So skittish had the interviewee been when approached on the subject of women in his life, that the writer postulated that it was her personal conviction that somewhere along the way Devereaux had been terribly hurt by someone he loved deeply. . . . And here, Ginevra winced. The writer concluded her character portrait with a disturbing synthesis: "Devereaux, his concert career floundering, appears to be searching for answers. But he's not looking in the direction of God. Like many, if not most, Europeans of our time, he appears to be almost totally secular; thus he has nowhere but within himself upon which to draw strength and inspiration. Sadly, his inner wells appear to retain only shallow reservoirs from which to draw. . . . A pity."

A nagging thought returned to tug at her heartstrings: What had *she* done—what had she *ever* done—to show Michael a better way? . . . "But," she retorted, "I don't want him to become a Christian just for *me!*" But this time that oft-used cop out didn't suffice. She kept seeing that stern-faced judge within. . . . In the long, long silence that followed was born a plan of action. If it worked, if he responded as she hoped he might, sooner or later, she would *know!* For inescapably, the secret would "out" through his music.

She determined to implement her plan of action that very day.

Several weeks after Ginevra's decision, Michael had returned to his hotel after a concert, a particularly unsatisfactory one—and it seemed these days that there were more and more of this kind. Even the crowd had been smaller than any he could remember in years. He was increasingly convinced that his career and life were both failures—and that there was little reason to remain living. He went to bed and vainly tried to sleep. After an hour or two of thrashing around, he got up, turned on the light, and looked for the last packet of mail forwarded to him by his agent. There was something in it that intrigued him. Ah! Here it was.

A small registered package had arrived from New York. There was no return address, and he didn't recognize the handwriting on the mailer. Inside was a slim, evidently long-out-of-print book titled *The Other Wise Man* written by an author he had never heard of: Henry Van Dyke. . . . Well, it looked like a quick read and he couldn't sleep anyhow . . .

A quick read it was not. He found himself rereading certain passages several times. It was after three o'clock in the morning when he finally put it down. He was moved in spite of himself. Then, he retired, this time to sleep.

During that Christmas season, he reread it twice more—and each time he read it, he wondered what had motivated that unknown person to send it.

Three months later came another registered packet from New York. It too was obviously a book and, to his joy, another old one. To his relief—for he had an intense fear of God and religion—it did not appear to be a religious book. The author and title were alike unknown to him: Myrtle Reed's *The Master's Violin*. The exquisite metallic lamination of this turn-of-the-century first edition quite took his breath away. *Someone* had spent some money on *this* gift! He read it that night, and it seemed, in some respects, that the joy and pain he vicariously experienced in the reading mirrored his own. And the violin! It brought back memories of that melody, that melody which just would not let him go, that melody which represented the high tide of his life.

It was mid-June, three months later, when the next registered package arrived from New York. This time, his hands were actually trembling as he opened the package. Another book by yet another author he'd never heard of: Harold Bell Wright. Kind of a strange title it had: *That Printer of Udel's*. But it was old and had a tipped-in cover: the combination was irresistible. He dropped everything and started to read.

He was not able to put it down. In it he saw depicted a portrait of Christian living unlike any he had ever seen before: a way of life that had to do not just with sterile doctrine but with a living, loving outreach to one's fellow man. He finished the book late that night. A month later, he read it again.

By late September, he had been watching his mail with great anticipation for some time. What would it be this time? Then it came: another book, first published in 1907, by the same author, with the intriguing title *The Calling of Dan Matthews*. It made the same impact upon him its predecessor had. Nevertheless, Michael was no easy nut to crack: he continued to keep his jury sequestered—he was nowhere near ready for a verdict of any kind.

Early in December arrived his second Van Dyke: *The Mansion*, a lovely lime-green illustrated edition. This book spawned some exceedingly disturbing questions about his inner motivations. Of what value, really, was *his* life? When was the last time he had ever done anything for someone without expecting something in return? For such a small book, it certainly stirred up some difficult-to-answer questions!

March brought a book he had often talked about reading but never had the temerity to tackle: Victor Hugo's forbidding *Les Miserables*: almost 1,500 pages unabridged! He wondered: *Why*? Why such a literary classic following what he had been sent before? He didn't wonder long: the story of Jean Valjean was a story of redemption: the story of a man who climbed out of hell. The first Christ-figure he could ever remember seeing in French literature. By now, he was beginning to look for fictional characters who exhibited, in some manner, Christian values.

At the end of the book was a brief note:

He did . . . but he felt terribly abused, sorely missing the expected package in June.

By the time September's leaves began to fall, he was in a state of intense longing. Certainly, after *Les Miserables*, and after a half-year wait, it would have to be a blockbuster! To his amazement and disgust, it was a slim mass-market paperback with the thoroughly unappetizing title of *Mere Christianity*. The author he knew of but had never read: C. S. Lewis.

Swallowing his negative feelings with great difficulty, he gingerly tested with his toes . . . Lewis's Jordan River. As he stepped farther in, he was—quite literally—overwhelmed. Every argument he had ever thrown up as a barrier between him and God was systematically and thoroughly demolished. He had had no idea that God and Christianity were any more than an amalgamation of feelings—for the first time, he was able to conceptualize God with his *mind*!

Whoever was sending him the books was either feeling sorry for making him wait so long—or punishing him by literally burying him in print! He was kindly given two weeks to digest *Mere Christianity* and then began the nonstop barrage of his soul. First came three shells in a row: Lewis's Space Trilogy: *Out of the Silent Planet*, *Perelandra*, and *That Hideous Strength*. At first, Michael, like so many other readers of these books, enjoyed the plot solely on the science fiction level. Then, he wryly observed to himself that Lewis had set him up: woven into the story was God and His plan of salvation!

The trilogy was followed by Lewis's *Screwtape Letters*. How Michael laughed as he read this one! How incredibly wily is the Great Antagonist! And how slyly Lewis had reversed the roles in order to shake up all his simplistic assumptions about the battles between Good and Evil.

A week later: another shell—*The Four Loves*. In it, Michael found himself reevaluating almost all of his people-related friendships in life. That was but the beginning: then Lewis challenged him to explore the possibilities of a friendship with the Eternal.

Two shells then came in succession: *Surprised by Joy* and *A Grief Observed*. At long last, he was able to learn more about Lewis the man. Not only that, but how Lewis, so late in life introduced to the joys of nuptial love, related to the untimely death of his bride. How Lewis, in his wracking grief, almost lost his way—almost turned away from God Himself! Paralleling Lewis's searing loss of his beloved was Michael's loss of Ginevra: relived once again, it was bone-wrenching in its intensity. More so than Lewis's—for he had not Lewis's God to turn to in the darkest hour.

The final seven shells came in the form of what appeared to be, at first glance, a series of books for children: Lewis's Chronicles of Narnia. It took Michael some time to figure out why he'd been sent this series last—after such heavyweights! It was not until he was about halfway through that he knew. By then, he had fully realized just how powerful a manifestation of the attributes of Christ Aslan the lion was. By the moving conclusion of *The Last Battle*, the fifteen shells from Lewis's howitzer had made mere rubble out of what was left of Michael's defense system.

Then came a beautiful edition of the Phillips translation

of the New Testament. On the flyleaf, in neat black calligraphy, was this line:

MAY THIS BOOK HELP TO MAKE YOUR NEW YEAR TRULY NEW.

He read the New Testament with a receptive attitude, taking a month to complete it. One morning, following a concert the night before in Florence, he rose very early and walked to the Arno River to watch the sunrise. As he leaned against a lamppost, his thoughts (donning their accountant coats) did an audit of the past three years.

He was belatedly discovering that a life without God just wasn't worth living: in fact, *nothing*, he now concluded, had any lasting meaning divorced from a higher power. He looked around him, mentally scrutinizing the lives of family members, friends, and colleagues in the music world. He noted the devastating divorce statistics, the splintered homes, and the resulting flotsam of loneliness and despair. Without God, he now concluded, no human relationship was likely to last very long.

Nevertheless, even now that he was thoroughly convinced—in his mind—that God represented the only way out of his dead-end existence, he bullheadedly balked at crossing the line out of the Dark into the Light.

The day before Easter of that tenth year, there came another old book, an expensive English first edition of Francis Thompson's poems. Inside, on the endsheet, was this coda to their faceless three-year friendship:

Dear Michael,
For almost three years now,
you have never been out of my
thoughts and prayers.
I hope that these books have come
to mean to you what they do to me.
This is your last book.
Please read "The Hound of Heaven."
The rest is up to you.
Your Friend

Immediately, he turned to the long poem and immersed himself in Thompson's lines. Although some of the words were a bit antiquated and jarred a little, nevertheless he felt that the lines were written laser-straight to him, especially those near the poem's gripping conclusion—for Michael identified totally with Thompson's own epic flight from the pursuing celestial Hound:

Whom will you find to love ignoble thee
    Save Me, save only Me?
All which I took from thee I did but take,
    Not for thy harms,
But just that thou might'st seek it in My arms.
    All which thy child's mistake
Fancies as lost, I have stored for thee at home.
    Rise, clasp My hand, and come!

These lines broke him . . . and he fell to his knees.

It was the morning after, and Michael awakened to the first Easter of the rest of his life. Needing very much to be alone, he decided to head for the family chalet near Mont Blanc. How fortunate, he mused, that the rest of the family was skiing at Saint Moritz that week.

Two hours before he got there, it began to snow, but his Porsche, itself born during a bitterly cold German winter, growled its delight as it devoured the road to Chamonix. It was snowing even harder when he arrived at the chalet, where Michael was greeted with delight by Jacques and Marie, the caretakers.

Breakfast was served adjacent to a roaring fire in the great alpine fireplace. Afterward, thoroughly satisfied, he leaned back in his favorite chair and looked out at the vista of falling snow.

He *felt*, he finally concluded, as if sometime in the night he had been reborn. It was as if all his life he had been carrying a staggeringly heavy backpack, a backpack into which some cruel overseer had dropped yet another five-pound brick *each* January 1 of his life, for as far back as he could remember. And now—suddenly—he was *free*! What a paradoxical revelation that was: that the long-feared surrender to God resulted in—not the dreaded strait-jacketed servitude—but the most incredible euphoric freedom he had ever imagined!

Looking back at the years of his life, he now recognized that he had been fighting God every step of the way, but God, refusing to give up on him, had merely kept His distance. He went to his suitcase, reached for that already precious book of poems, returned to his seat by the fire, and turned again to that riveting first stanza:

I fled Him, down the nights and down the days;
  I fled Him, down the arches of the years;
  I fled Him, down the labyrinthine ways

Of my own mind, and in the midst of tears
I hid from Him, and under running laughter.
  Up vistaed hopes I sped;
  And shot, precipitated
Adown Titanic glooms of chastened fears,
  From those strong Feet that followed, followed
    after.
But with unhurrying chase,
  And unperturbed pace,
Deliberate speed, majestic instancy,
  They beat—and a Voice beat
  More instant than the Feet—
"All things betray thee, who betrayest Me!"

He turned away, unable, because of a blurring of his vision, to read on.

"How many *years* I have lost!" he sighed.

Years during which the frenetic pace of his life caused the Pursuing Hound to sadly drop back. Years during which he proudly strutted, wearing the tinsel crown of popularity. And then . . . that flimsy bit of ephemera was taken away and the long descent into the maelstrom had taken place. And it had been in his darkest hour, when he actually felt Ultimate Night reaching for him, that he plainly and distinctly heard his Pursuer again.

For almost three years now that Pursuer had drawn ever closer. There had been a strange meshing: the Voice in the crucifixion earthquake who spoke to Artaban, the Power that defied the Ally in the Dan Matthews story, the Force revealed through the pulsating strings of "mine Cremona," the Presence which—through the Bishop's incredible act

of forgiveness and compassion—saved the shackled life of Jean Valjean, the Angel who showed John Weightman's pitiful mansion to him, Malacandra of the Perelandra story, and Aslan in the Narnia series. As he read "The Hound of Heaven," all the foregoing lost their distinctiveness and merged into the pursuing Hound. They were one and the same!

Michael resonated with a strange new power, a power he had never experienced before. It was as if, during the night, in his badly crippled power station (a generating facility to which, over the years, one incoming line after another had been cut, until he was reduced to but one frail piece of frayed wire that alone kept him from blackout), a new cable, with the capacity to illuminate an entire world, had been snaked down the dusty stairs, and then: *plugged in.*

Then—from far back (even before his descent into hell), two images emerged out of the mists of time: one visual and one aural: the tear-stained face of the Only Woman . . . and the throbbing notes of "Meditation."

Tingling all over, he stood up and walked over to the grand piano always kept in the lodge for his practicing needs, lifted up the lid, seated himself on the bench, and looked up. Humbly, he asked the question: "Am I ready at last, Lord?"

Then he reached for the keys and began to play. As his fingers swept back and forth, something else occurred: for the first time in over nine years, he was able—without printed music—to replay in his mind every note, every intonation, he and Ginevra had heard in that far-off bell tower of Votivkirche. Not only

that . . . but the sterility was gone! The current that had been turned on inside him leaped to his hands and fingers.

At *last* . . . he was ready.

* * * * *

Michael immediately discarded the fall concert repertoire, chosen as it had been merely for showmanship reasons, and substituted a new musical menu for the old. Ever so carefully, as a master chef prepares a banquet for royalty, he selected his individual items. In fact, he agonized over them, for each number must not only mesh with all the others, but enhance as well, gradually building into a crescendo that would trumpet a musical vision of his new life.

Much more complicated was the matter of his new recording. How could he stop the process at such a late date? Not surprisingly, when he met with Polygram management and dropped his bombshell, they were furious. Only with much effort was he able to calm them down—and that on a premise they strongly doubted: that his replacement would be so much *better* that they would be more than compensated for double the expected production expense!

He walked out of their offices in a very subdued mood. If he had retained any illusions about how low his musical stock had sunk, that meeting would have graphically settled the question. If his new recording failed to sell well, he would almost certainly be dropped from the label.

Then, he memorized all the numbers before making his trial run recording; this way, he was able to give his undivided attention to interpretation before wrapping up the

process. Only after he himself was thoroughly satisfied with the results did he have it recorded and then hand-carried by his agent to Deutsche Gramophone/Polygram management.

He didn't have to wait very long; only minutes after they played his pilot recording, Michael received a long-distance phone call from the president himself. Michael had known him for years and knew him to be a very tough hombre indeed. Recognizing full well that he and the company lived and died by the bottom line, he was used to making decisions for the most pragmatic of reasons. And recording artists feared him because he had a way of telling the unvarnished truth sans embellishments or grace-notes. And now he was on the line. Initially, almost speechless, he finally recovered and blurted out, "What has happened, Michael? For years now, your recordings have seemed—pardon my candidness, but you know blunt me—a bit tinny, fluffy, sometimes listless, and even a bit . . . uh . . . for want of a better word: "peevish," more or less as if you were irritably going through the motions again, but with little idea why. Now, here, on the other hand, comes a recording which sounded to us like you woke up one morning and decided to belatedly take control of your life and career; that there were new and exciting ways of interpreting music—interpreting with power . . . and beauty . . . and, I might add, Michael . . . a promise of depth and seasoning we quite frankly no longer believed was in you! *What has happened?*"

That incredible summer passed in a blur of activity. The long ebb over at last, the incoming tidal forces of Michael's life now thundered up the beaches of the musical world. Deutsche Gramophone management and employees worked around the clock to process, release, and then market what they firmly believed would be the greatest recording of his career. Word leaked out even before it was released; consequently, there was a run on it when it hit the market. All of this translated into enthusiastic interest in his fall concert schedule.

Early in August, before the recording had been released, Michael phoned his New York agent, who could hardly contain himself about the new bookings which were flooding in for the North American tour, spring of the following year. Michael, after first swearing him to secrecy, told him that he was entrusting to his care the most delicate assignment of their long association—one which, if botched, would result in irreparable damage. The agent promised to fulfill his instructions to the letter.

He wanted of him three things: to trace the whereabouts of a certain lady (taking great pains to ensure that the lady in question would not be aware of the search process); to find out if the lady had married; to process a mailing (the contents of the mailing would be adjusted according to whether the lady had married or not).

* * * * *

Meanwhile, Ginevra played the waiting game—a very *hard* game to play without great frustration. And for her, the frustration level had been steadily building for almost three years. *When* would she know?

Within a year after mailing her first book, she felt reasonably confident that he was reading what she had sent, but she had little data upon which to base her assumptions.

During the second year, little snips of information relating to possible change in Devereaux appeared here and there. Nothing really significant, but enough to give her hope.

She had knelt down by her bed that memorable morning before she mailed Thompson's poems. In her heartfelt supplication, she voiced her conviction that, with this book, she had now done all that was in her power to do. The rest was up to Him. Then she drove down the mountain to the Boulder post office and sent it to her New York relayer—and returned home to wait.

It was several months before the Devereaux-related excitement in the music world began to build. Her heart beat a lilting "allegro" the day she first heard about the growing interest in Michael's new recording. She could hardly wait to get a copy.

Then came the day when, in her mailbox, there appeared a little yellow piece of paper indicating that a registered piece of mail was waiting for her in the post office. It turned out to be a *very large* package from an unknown source in New York.

Not until she had returned to her chalet did she open it. Initially, she was almost certain that one of her former students was playing a joke on her, for, the box was disproportionately light. She quickly discovered the reason: it was jammed full of wadded-up paper. Her room was half full of paper before she discovered the strange-shaped box at the very bottom of the mailing carton. . . . *What* could it be? . . . *Who* could it be from? . . . In this box, obviously packed with great care, were five items, each separated by a hard cardboard divider: a perfect flame-red rose in a sealed moisture-tight container, Michael's new Deutsche Gramophone recording, a publicity poster of a concert program, which read as follows:

MICHAEL DEVEREAUX
FIRST CHRISTMAS EVE CONCERT
VIENNA OPERA HOUSE

(followed by the other data giving exact time and date), a round-trip airline ticket to Vienna, and at the very bottom, in an exquisite gold box—a front section ticket to the concert.

*   *   *   *   *

Fearing lest someone in the Standing section take her place before she could reach her seat, during the enthusiastic applause following Bach's "Italian Concerto," Ginevra asked an usher to escort her to her seat in the third row. Michael, who had turned to acknowledge the applause, caught the motion: the beautiful woman coming down the aisle. And she was wearing a flame-red rose. Even in Vienna, a city known for its beautiful women, she was a sight to pin dreams on.

How terribly grateful he was to the audience for continuing to clap, for that gave him time, precious time in which to restore his badly damaged equilibrium. It was passing strange, mused Michael. For years now, both his greatest dream and his greatest nightmare were one and the same: that Ginevra would actually show up for one of his concerts. The nightmare had to do with deep-seated fear that her presence in the audience would inevitably destroy his concentration, and with it the concert itself. And now,

here she was! If he ever needed a higher power, he needed it now. Briefly, he bowed his head. When he raised it, he felt again this new sense of serenity, peace, and command.

Leaving the baroque world of Bach, he now turned to César Franck; being a composer of romantic music, but with baroque connections, Michael had felt him to be a perfect bridge from Bach to Martin and Prokofiev. As he began to play Franck's "Prelude: Chorale et Fugue," he settled down to making this the greatest concert of his career. He had sometimes envied the great ones their announced conviction that, for each, the greatest concert was always the very next one on the schedule—they *never* took a free ride on their laurels. Only this season it had been that he had joined the masters, belatedly recognizing that the greatest thanks he could ever give his Maker would be to extend his powers to the limits, every time he performed, regardless of how large or how small the crowd.

The opera house audience had quickly recognized the almost mind-boggling change in attitude. The last time he had played here, reviewers had unkindly but accurately declared him washed up. So desperate for success of any kind had he become that he openly pandered to what few people still came. It was really pathetic: he would edge out onto the platform like an abused puppy, cringing lest he be kicked again. Not surprisingly, what he apparently expected, he got.

Now, there was never any question as to who was in control. On the second, he would stride purposefully onto the stage, with a pleasant look on his face, and gracefully bow. He would often change his attire between sections: adding a visual extra to the auditory. His attire was always impeccable: newly cleaned and pressed, and he was neither over- nor underdressed for the occasion.

But neither was he proud, recognizing just how fragile is the line between success and failure—and how terribly difficult it is to stay at the top once you get there. Nor did he anymore grovel or play to the galleries. The attitude he now projected was, quite simply: *I'm so pleased you honored me by coming out tonight. I have prepared long and hard for this occasion; consequently, it is both my intent and my expectation that we shall share the greatest musical hour and a half of our lifetimes.*

Ginevra felt herself becoming part of a living, breathing island in time. Every concert performed well, is that: kind of a magic moment during which outside life temporarily ceases to be. Great music after all, is outside of time and thus not subject to its rules. Thus it was that Ginevra, like the Viennese audience, lost all sense of identity as Devereaux's playing became all the reality they were to know for some time.

These weren't just notes pried from a reluctant piano they were hearing: this was life itself, life with all its frustrations and complexities.

With such power and conviction did César Franck speak from the grave that they stood applauding for three minutes at the end of the first half. In fact, disregarding opera house protocol, a number of the younger members of the audience swarmed onto the stage and surrounded Michael before he could get backstage. The new Michael stopped, and with a pleasant look on his face all the while, autographed every last program that was shoved at him. Nay—more than that: as one of these autograph seekers, jubilant of face, came back to Ginevra's row, she saw him

proudly showing the program to his parents. Michael had taken the trouble to learn each person's name so he could inscribe each one personally!

Michael's tux was wringing wet. As for the gleaming black Boersendorfer, with such superhuman energy had Michael attacked it that it begged for the soothing balm of a piano tuner's ministrations; hence it was wheeled out for a badly needed rest. In its place was the monarch of the city's Steinway grands. Michael had specifically requested this living nine feet of history. No one knew for sure just how old it was, but it had for years been the pride and joy of Horowitz. Rubinstein would play here on no other, and it was even rumored that the great Paderewski performed on it. Michael, like all real artists, deeply loved his favorite instruments. Like the fabled Velveteen Rabbit, when an instrument such as this Steinway has brought so much happiness, fulfillment, meaning, and love into life . . . well, over the years, it ceases to be just a piano and approaches personhood. Thus it was that Michael, before it was wheeled in, had a heart-to-heart chat with it.

A stagehand, watching the scene, didn't even lift an eyebrow—concert musicians were *all* a loony bunch.

Only after a great deal of soul-searching had Michael decided to open the second half of his concert with Swiss-born Frank Martin's "Eight Preludes." He had long appreciated and loved Martin's fresh approach to music, his lyrical euphonies. Martin reminded Michael of the American composer Howard Hanson. He often had a difficult time choosing which one to include in a given repertoire; but this season, it was Martin's turn.

More and more sure of himself, Michael only gained in power as he retold Martin's story; by the time he finished the Preludes, he owned Vienna. The deafening applause rolled on and on. And nobody appeared willing to ever sit down.

Finally, the house quiet once again, a microphone was brought out and Michael stepped up to speak.

"Ladies and gentlemen," he began, "I have a substitution to make. As you know, I am scheduled to perform Prokofiev's Sonata number 6 in A Major, opus 82, as my concluding number, but I hope you will not be *too* disappointed"—and here he smiled his boyish grin—"if I substitute a piece that I composed, a piece that has never before been performed in public."

He paused, then continued: "Ten years ago tonight, in this fair city, this piece of music was born, but it was not completed until late this spring. I have been saving it for tonight." And here, he dared to glance in the direction of Ginevra.

"The title is . . . 'Variations on a Theme by Massenet.' "

Nothing in Michael's composing experience had been more difficult than deciding what to do with "Meditation." And the difficulties did not fall away with his conversion. He still had some tough decisions to face: Should his variations consist merely as creative side-trips from that one melodic base? By doing so, he knew he could dazzle. Should the variations be limited to musical proof that he and his Maker were now friends? With neither was he satisfied.

Of all the epiphanies he had ever experienced, none could compare with the one which was born to him one "God's in His Heaven / All's right with the world" spring morning: He realized that he could create a counterpart to what Massenet had done with the "Meditation" intermezzo: a fusion of earthly love with the divine. Belatedly, he recognized a great truth: God does not come to us in the abstract—He comes to us through flesh and blood. We do not initially fall in love with God as a principle; rather, we first fall in love with human beings whose lives radiate friendship with the divine. It is only *then* that we seek out God on our own.

Ginevra was such a prototype—that is why he had fallen in love with her. And he had little doubt in his mind but that it was she who had choreographed his conversion. No one else had he ever known who would have cared enough to institute and carry out such a flawless plan of action. Besides, some of the book choices made him mighty suspicious.

Michael had also recognized what all true artists do sooner or later: that their greatest work must come from within, from known experience. If he was to endow his variations with power akin to the original, they must emanate from the joys and sorrows that made him what he

was . . . and since she and God were inextricably woven together in Michael's multi-hued bolt of life, then woven together they must remain throughout the composition.

It would not be acceptable for her to distance herself and pretend she could judge what he had become dispassionately. No, Ginevra must enter into the world he had composed . . . and decide at the other end whether or not she would stay.

In Ginevra's mind, everything seemed to harken back to that cold night in the tower of Votivkirche, for it was there that two lives, only hours from oneness, had seen the cable of their intertwining selves unravel in only seconds.

Furthermore, there was more than God holding them apart. More than her romanticism as compared to his realism. That far-off exchange of words had highlighted for her some significant problems which, left unresolved, would preclude marriage even if Michael *had* been converted. Let's see: How could she conceptualize them?

Essentially, it all came down to these. Michael had laughed at and ridiculed her deepest-felt feelings. Had made light of her tears. Had shown a complete absence of empathy. Worse yet, he exhibited a clear-cut absence of the one most crucial character trait in the universe: *kindness.* Also, at no time since she had known him had she ever seen him admit in any way that he was wrong about anything—and compounding the problem, he had refused to disclose his true identity to her:

There had been a locked door halfway down to his heart.

There had been another locked door halfway up to his soul.

As far as she knew, both doors were still closed.

But if they ever *were* to be unlocked . . . "Meditation" would be the key.

* * * * *

As-soft-as-a-mother's-touch pianissimo, Michael begins to play. So softly that there appear to be no breaks at all between the notes, but rather a continuous skein of melodic sound. And, for the first time in Michael's career, there is a flowing oneness with the piano: impossible to tell where flesh, blood, and breath end and where wood, ivory, and metal join.

Ginevra cannot help but feel tense in spite of blurred fingers weaving dreams around her. Deep down, she knows that what occurs during *this* piece of music will have a profound effect upon the rest of her life. And the rest of Michael's life.

But she hadn't traveled so many thousands of miles just to be a referee or a critic. If their two worlds are ever to be one, she must leave her safe seat in the audience and step into the world of Michael's composition. Strangely enough—and living proof that it is the "small" things in life that are often the most significant—Michael's exhibition of kindness to the young people who blocked his exit during intermission strongly predisposes her in his favor.

How beautifully his arpeggios flow, cascading as serenely as alpine brooks singing their way down to the sea. All nature appears to be at peace. As Michael plays, she can envision the birds' wake-up calls, the falling rain and drifting snow, the sighing of her dear pines, and the endless journey of the stars. The world is a beautiful place . . . and love is in the air.

Suddenly, she stiffens: certainly those are bells she is hearing. Yes: Christmas bells, flooding the universe with joy. She listens intently as their pealing grows ever louder—then *that theme*! It begins to mesh with the bells, but only for an instant. Right in the middle of it, there is an ominous shift from major to minor key, and from harmony to dissonance. And the bells! In that self-same instant, the pealing joy ceases and is replaced by tolling sorrow. How uncannily perfect is Michael's capture of that moment— that moment when all the joy in their world went sour.

The dissonance and tolling eventually give way to a classical music potpourri. Here and there she recognizes snatches of well-known themes, some of them from piano concertos. But the notes are clipped off short and played perfunctorily: more or less as if the pianist doesn't much care how they sound as long as they all get played in record time. Several times, the Theme tries to edge in, but each time it is rudely repulsed.

Now it is that Dvorak's "New World Symphony" thunders in. Aha! At last: some resolution! Some affirmation! Not so. It quickly becomes apparent that this paean to a brave new world is, ironically, in steady retreat instead of advancing to triumph. Almost—it seems to her—as if it were a retrograde "Bolero": its theme progressively diminishing in power instead of increasing. Once again, "Meditation" seeks entry; once again, it is unceremoniously disposed of.

By now, Ginevra is deciphering Michael's musical code quite well: vividly revealed has been the progressive deterioration of Michael both as a person and as a pianist. From the moment in the cathedral tower when the bells began to toll, every variation that followed has dealt with the stages of his fall.

Then, clouds close in, thunder rumbles in the east, lightning strikes short-circuit the sky, and the rain falls. Torrents of it. Darkness sweeps in, and with it all the hells loose on this turbulent planet. Ginevra shivers as Michael stays in minor keys, mourning all the sadness and pain in the universe.

The winds gradually increase to hurricane strength. Far ahead of her—for she is exposed to the elements too—she sees Michael, almost out of sight in the gloom, retreating from the storm. She follows, and attempts to call to him, but to no avail. The tempest swallows the words before they can be formed. Then the black clouds close in . . . and she loses sight of him altogether.

As the hurricane reaches ultimate strength, major keys are in full flight from the minors (Ginevra discovered some time back that Michael is equating majors with the forces of Light, and minors with the forces of Darkness). It does not seem possible that any force on earth could save Michael from destruction.

It is now, in the darkest midnight, when the few majors left are making their last stand. She senses that, for Michael, the end is near. Now, when she has all but conceded victory to the Dark Power, she again hears the strains of *Thaïs*'s Theme! How can such a frail thing possibly survive when leagued against the legions of Darkness? But, almost unbelievably, it does.

At this instant, Ginevra chances to look with wide-open eyes at—not Michael the pianist but Michael the man. He has clearly forgotten all about the world, the concert audience, even *her*. In his total identification with the struggle for his soul, he is playing for only two people: himself—the penitent sinner—and God. And his face? Well, never afterwards could she really explain, but one thing was absolutely certain: there before her . . . was Michael's naked soul.

With Michael's surrender, the tide turns at last: The storm rages on, but the enemy is now unmistakably in retreat. Dissonance and minors contest every step of the battlefield, trying vainly to hold off the invading Light. Then victorious majors begin sweeping the field.

Ginevra discovers in all this a great truth: it is minors that reveal the full beauty of majors. Had she not heard "Meditation" sobbing on the ropes of a minor key, she would never have realized the limitless power of God. It is the minor key that gives texture and beauty to the major; and it is dissonance that, by contrast, reveals the glory of harmony. . . . It is sorrow that brings our wandering feet back to God. . . .

Finally, with the mists beginning to dissipate and the sun to break through, the Theme reappears, but alone for the first time. Now it is that Ginevra feels the full upward pull of the music, for "Meditation" soars heavenward with such passion, pathos, and power that gravity is powerless to restrain it.

And Ginevra . . . her choice made . . . reaches up,
and with Michael,
climbs the stairs of heaven to God.

The Littlest Orphan and the Christ Baby

Margaret E. Sangster

This past year has been beyond traumatic; thus, we were most receptive when our Pacific Press publisher suggested we take a retrospective pause, look back through the years, and share the behind-the-scenes story of Christmas in My Heart® *(also carried by Focus on the Family and Tyndale House, Doubleday Random House, Howard/Simon & Schuster, plus many translating publishers).*

Dale Galusha (president of Pacific Press® Publishing Association) invited me to share with our readers some insights into our first seasons: What kind of reader responses have we received over the years? Pick a story out of each collection and tell our readers your reasons for choosing that story to include in this collection.

The release of 1993 brought surprises: Christmas in My Heart *was now graced by a bright green cover (the first had been white). It bravely bore a "2" on the cover and spine. Dr. James Dobson honored two stories (Frederic Loomis's "The Tiny Foot" and Cathy Miller's "Delayed Delivery") by making them Focus on the Family Christmas Stories of the Year.*

Of the seventeen stories in book 2, one of them, "The Littlest Orphan and the Christ Baby," was one of my mother's favorite Christmas stories in her public story readings. My two siblings (Romayne and Marjorie) and I knew our mother's favorite stories almost by heart—including this one. Not to worry: we'd cry along with the audience when Mom reached the heart-tugging conclusion.

* * * * *

The Littlest Orphan gazed up into the face of the Christ Baby, who hung gilt-framed and smiling above the mantel shelf. The mantel was dark, made of a black, mottled marble that suggested tombstones, and the long room, despite its rows of neat, white beds, gave an impression of darkness, too. But the picture above the mantel sparkled and scintillated and threw off an aura of sheer happiness. Even the neat "In Memoriam" card tacked to the wall directly under it could not detract from its joy. All of rosy babyhood, all of unspoiled laughter, all of the beginnings of life were in that picture! And the Littlest Orphan sensed it, even though he did not quite understand.

The Matron was coming down the room with many wreaths, perhaps a dozen of them, braceleting her thin arm. The wreaths were just a trifle dusty, their imitation holly leaves spoke plaintively of successive years of hard usage. But it was only two days before Christmas and the wreaths would not show up so badly under artificial light. The board of trustees, coming for the entertainment on Christmas Eve, never arrived until the early winter dusk

33

had settled down. And the wreaths could be laid away, as soon as the holiday was past, for another 12 months.

The Littlest Orphan, staring up at the picture, did not hear the Matron's approaching footsteps. True, the Matron wore rubber heels—but any other orphan in the whole asylum would have heard her. Only the Littlest Orphan, with his thin, sensitive face and his curious fits of absorption, could have ignored her coming. He started painfully as her sharp voice cut into the silence.

"John," she said, and the frost that made such pretty lacework upon the window pane wrought havoc with her voice: *John, what are you doing here?*

The Littlest Orphan answered after the manner of all small boy-children. "Nothin'!" he said.

Standing before him, the Matron—who was a large woman—seemed to tower. "You are not telling the truth, John," she said. "You have no right to be in the dormitory at this hour. Report to Miss Mace at once" (Miss Mace was the primary teacher) "and tell her that I said you were to write five pages in your copybook. *At once!*"

With hanging head the Littlest Orphan turned away. It seemed terribly unfair, although it was against the rules to spend any but sleeping hours in the dormitory! He was just learning to write, and five pages meant a whole afternoon of cramped fingers and tired eyes. But how could he explain to this grim woman that the Christ Baby fascinated him, charmed him, and comforted him? How could he explain that the Christ Baby's wide eyes had a way of glancing down, almost with understanding, into his own? How could he tell, with the few weak words of his vocabulary, that he loved the Christ Baby, whose smile was so tenderly sweet? That he spent much of his time standing, as he stood now, in the shadow of that smile? He trudged away with never a word, down the length of the room, his clumsy shoes making a feeble clatter on the bare boards of the floor. When he was almost at the door, the Matron called after him.

"Don't drag your feet, John!" she commanded. And so he walked the rest of the way on tiptoe. And closed the door very softly after him.

* * * * *

The halls had already been decorated with long streamers of red and green crepe paper that looped along, in a half-hearted fashion, from picture to picture. The stair railing was wound with more of the paper, and the schoolroom, where Miss Mace sat stiffly behind a broad desk, was vaguely brightened by red cloth poinsettias set here and there at random. But the color of them was not reflected in the Littlest Orphan's heart as he delivered his message and received in return a battered copybook.

As he sat at his desk, and writing laboriously about the cat who ate the rat and the dog who ran after the cat, he could hear the other orphans playing outside in the courtyard. Always they played from four o'clock, when school was over, until five-thirty, which was suppertime. It was a rule to play from four to five-thirty. They were running and shouting together, but in a stilted way.

The Littlest Orphan did not envy them much. They were all older and stronger than he, and their games were sometimes hard to enjoy. He had been the last baby taken before a new ruling, making six years the minimum entrance age, had gone through. And he was only five years old now. Perhaps it was his very littleness that made the Matron more intolerant of him—he presented to her a problem that could not be met in a mass way. His clothing had to be several sizes smaller than the other clothing; his lessons less advanced. And so on.

Drearily he wrote. And listened, between sentences, to the scratching pen of Miss Mace . . . The dog had caught the cat. And now the man beat the dog. And then it was time to start all over again, back at the place where the cat ate the rat. Two pages, three pages, four pages . . . Surreptitiously the Littlest Orphan moved his fingers, one by one, and wondered that he was still able to move them. Then, working slowly, he finished the last page and handed the copy book back to the teacher. As she studied it, her face softened slightly.

"Why did the Matron punish you, John?" she asked, as if on impulse, as she made a correction in a sentence.

The Littlest Orphan hesitated for a second. And then: "I shouldn't have been in the dormitory," he said slowly. "An' I was!"

Again Miss Mace asked a question.

"But what," she queried, "were you doing there? Why weren't you out playing with the other children?"

She didn't comment upon the fault, but the Littlest Orphan knew that she, also, thought the punishment rather severe. Only it isn't policy to criticize a superior's method of discipline. She answered her second question gravely.

"I was lookin' at th' Christ Baby over the mantel," he said.

As if to herself, Miss Mace spoke. "You mean the picture Mrs. Benchly gave in memory of her son," she murmured, "the pastel." And then, "Why were you looking at it—" She hesitated, and the Littlest Orphan didn't know that she had almost said "dear."

Shyly the child spoke, and wistfulness lay across his thin, small face—an unrealized wistfulness. "He looks so—nice—" said the Littlest Orphan gently, "like he had a mother, maybe."

* * * * *

Supper that night was brief, and after supper there were carols to practice in the assembly room. The Littlest Orphan, seated at the extreme end of the line, enjoyed the singing. The red-headed boy, who fought so often in the courtyard, had a high, thrilling soprano. Listening to him as he sang the solo parts made the Littlest Orphan forget a certain black eye, and a nose that had once been swollen and bleeding. Made him forget lonely hours when he had lain uncomforted in his bed, as a punishment for quarreling.

The red-headed boy was singing something about "gold and frank-kin-sense, and myrrh." The Littlest Orphan told himself that they must be very beautiful things. Gold—the Christ Baby's frame was of gold, but frank-kin-sense and myrrh were unguessed names. Maybe they were flowers, real flowers that smelled pretty, not red cloth ones. He shut his eyes, singing automatically, and imagined what these flowers looked like—the color and shape of their petals, and whether they grew on tall lily stalks or on short pansy stems. And then the singing was over and he opened his eyes with a start and realized that the Matron was speaking.

"Before you go to bed," she was saying, "I want you to understand that you must be on your good behavior until after the trustees leave tomorrow evening. You must not make any disorder in the corridors or in the dormitories—they have been especially cleaned and dusted. You must pay strict attention to the singing; the trustees like to hear you sing! They will all be here, even Mrs. Benchly, who has not visited us since her son died. And if one of you misbehaves—"

She stopped abruptly, but her silence was crowded with meaning, and many a child squirmed uncomfortably in his place. It was only after a moment that she spoke again.

"Good night!" she said abruptly.

And the orphans chorused back, "Good night."

* * * * *

Undressing carefully and swiftly, for the dormitory was cold and the gas lights were dim, the Littlest Orphan wondered about the trustees—and in particular about the Mrs. Benchly who had lost her son. All trustees were ogres to asylum children, but the Littlest Orphan couldn't help feeling that Mrs. Benchly was the least ogre-like of them all. Somehow she was a part of the Christ Baby's picture, and it was a part of her. If she were responsible for it, she could not be all bad! So ruminating, the Littlest Orphan said his brief prayers—any child who forgot his prayers was punished severely—and slid between the sheets into his bed.

Some orphans made a big lump under their bed covers. The red-headed boy was stocky, and so were others. Some of them were almost fat. But the Littlest Orphan made hardly any lump at all. The sheet, the cotton blanket, and the spread went over him with scarcely a ripple. Often the Littlest Orphan had wished that there might be another small boy who could share his bed—he took up such a tiny section of it. Another small boy would have made the bed seem warmer, somehow, and less lonely. Once two orphans had come to the asylum, and they were brothers. They had shared things—beds and desks and books. Maybe brothers were unusual gifts from a surprisingly blind providence, gifts that were granted only once in a hundred years! More rare, even, than mothers.

Mothers—the sound of the word had a strange effect upon the Littlest Orphan, even when he said it silently in his soul. It meant so much that he did not comprehend, so much for which he vaguely hungered. Mothers stood for warm arms, and kisses, and soft words. Mothers meant punishments, too, but gentle punishment that did not really come from away inside.

Often the Littlest Orphan had heard the rest talking stealthily about mothers. Some of them could actually remember having owned one! But the Littlest Orphan could not remember. He had arrived at the asylum as a baby, delicate and frail and too young for memories that would later come to bless him and to cause a strange, sharp sort of hurt. When the rest spoke of bedtime stories, and lullabies, and sugar cookies, he listened, wide-eyed and half-incredulous, to their halting sentences.

It was growing very cold in the dormitory, and it was dark. Even the faint flicker of light had been taken away. The Littlest Orphan wiggled his toes under the bottom blanket, and wished that sleep would come. Some nights it came quickly, but this night—perhaps he was overtired, and it was so cold!

As a matter of habit his eyes searched through the dark for the place where the Christ Baby hung. He could not distinguish even the dim outlines of the gilt frame, but he knew that the Christ Baby was rosy and chubby and smiling, that his eyes were deeply blue and filled with cheer. Involuntarily the Littlest Orphan stretched out his thin hands and dropped them back again against the spread. All about him the darkness lay like a smothering coat, and the Christ Baby, even though He smiled, was invisible. The other children were sleeping. All up and down the long room sounded their regular breathing, but the Littlest Orphan could not sleep. He wanted something that he was unable to define, wanted it with such a burning intensity that the tears crowded into his eyes. He sat up abruptly in his bed, a small, shivering figure with quivering lips and a baby ache in his soul that had never really known babyhood.

Loneliness—it swept about him. More disheartening than the cold. More enveloping than the darkness. There was no fear in him of the shadows in the corner, of the creaking shutters and the narrow stair. Such fears are discouraged early in children who live by rule and routine. No, it was a feeling more poignant than fear, a feeling that clutched at him and squeezed his small body until it was dry and shaking and void of expression.

Of all the sleeping dormitory full of children, the Littlest Orphan was the only child who knew the ache of such loneliness. Even the ones who had been torn away from family ties had, each one of them, something beautiful to keep preciously close. But the Littlest Orphan had nothing—nothing ... The loneliness filled him with a strange impulse, an impulse that sent him sliding over the edge of his bed with small arms outflung.

* * * * *

All at once he was crossing the floor on bare, mouse-quiet feet, past the placidly sleeping children, past the row of lockers, past the table with its neat cloth and black-bound, impressive guest book. Past everything until he stood, a white spot in the blackness, directly under the mantel. The Christ Baby hung above him. And, though the Littlest Orphan could not see, he felt that the blue eyes were looking down tenderly. All at once he wanted to touch the Christ Baby, to hold him tight, to feel the sweetness and warmth of Him. Tensely, still moved by the curious impulse, he tiptoed back to where the table stood. Carefully he laid the guest book on the floor; carefully he removed the white cloth. And then staggering under the, to him, great weight, he carried the table noiselessly back with him. Though it was really a small light table, the Littlest Orphan breathed hard as he set it down. He had to rest, panting, for a moment, before he could climb up on it.

All over the room lay silence, broken only by the sleepy sounds of the children. The Littlest Orphan listened almost prayerfully as he clambered upon the tabletop and drew himself to an erect position. His small hands groped along the mantel shelf, touched the lower edge of the gilt frame. But the Christ Baby was still out of reach.

Feverishly, obsessed with one idea, the Littlest Orphan raised himself on tiptoe. His hands gripped the chill marble of the mantel. Tugging, twisting—all with the utmost quiet—he pulled himself up until he was kneeling upon the mantel shelf. Quivering with nervousness as well as the now intense cold, he finally stood erect. And then, only then, was he able to feel the wire and nail that held the Christ Baby's frame against the wall. His numb fingers loosened the wire carefully. And then at last the picture was in his arms.

It was heavy, the picture. And hard. Not soft and warm as he had somehow expected it to be. But it was the Christ Baby, nevertheless. Holding it close, the Littlest Orphan fell to speculating upon the ways of getting down, now that both of his hands were occupied. It would be hard to slide from the mantel to the table, and from table to floor, with neither sound nor mishap.

His eyes troubled, his mouth a wavering line in his pinched face, the Littlest Orphan crowded back against the wall. The darkness held now the vague menace of depth. Destruction lurked in a single misstep. It had been a long way up. It would be even longer going down. And he had the Christ Baby, as well as himself, to care for.

Gingerly he advanced one foot over the edge of the mantel—and drew it back. Sharply. He almost screamed in sudden terror. It was as if the dark had reached out long, bony fingers to pull him from his place of safety. He wanted to raise his hands to his face, but he could not release his hold upon the gilt frame. All at once he realized that his hands were growing numb with the cold and that his feet were numb, too.

The minutes dragged by. Somewhere a clock struck, many times. The Littlest Orphan had never heard the clock strike so many times, at night, before. He cowered back until it seemed to his scared, small mind that he would sink into the wall. And then, as the clock ceased striking, he heard another sound—a sound that brought dread to his heart. It was a step in the hall, a heavy, firm step that, despite rubber heels, was now clearly recognizable. It would be the Matron, making her rounds of the building before she went to bed. As the steps came nearer along the hall, a light, soft and yellow, seemed to glow in the place. It would be the lamp that she carried in her hand.

The Matron reached the door—peered in. And then, with lamp held high, she entered the room. Her swift glance swept the row of white beds—each, but one, with its sleeping occupant.

The Littlest Orphan, on the mantel, clutched the Christ Baby closer in his arms. And waited. It seemed to him that his shivering must shake the room. He gritted his teeth convulsively, as the Matron's eyes found his tumbled, empty bed.

Hastily, forgetting to be quiet, the woman crossed the room. She pulled back the spread, the blanket. And then, as if drawn by a magnet, her eyes lifted, traveled across the room. And found the small, white figure that pressed back into the narrow space. Her voice was sharper even than her eyes when she spoke.

"John," she called abruptly, and her anger made her forget to be quiet. *What are you doing up there?*

Across the top of the Christ Baby's gilt frame, the eyes of the Littlest Orphan stared into the eyes of the Matron with something of the fascination that one sees in the eyes of a bird charmed by a cat or a snake. In narrow, white beds, all over the room, children were stirring, pulling themselves erect, staring. One child snickered behind a sheltering hand. But the Littlest Orphan was conscious only of the Matron. He waited for her to speak again. In a moment she did.

"John," she said, and her voice was burning, and yet chill, with rage, "you are a bad boy. *Come down at once!*"

His eyes blank with sheer fright, his arms clasping the picture close, the Littlest Orphan answered the tone of that voice. With quivering lips he advanced one foot, then the other. And stepped into the space that was the room below. He was conscious that some child screamed—he himself did not utter a sound. And that the Matron started forward. And then he struck the table and rolled with it, and the Christ Baby's splintering picture, into the darkness.

* * * * *

The Littlest Orphan spent the next day in bed, with an aching head and a wounded heart. The pain of his bruises did not make a great difference; neither did the threats of the Matron penetrate his consciousness. Only the bare space over the mantel mattered—only the blur of blue and yellow and red upon the hearth, where the pastel had struck. Only the knowledge that the Christ Baby, the meaning of all light and happiness, was no more, troubled him.

There was a pleasant stir about the asylum. An excited child, creeping into the dormitory, told the Littlest Orphan that one of the trustees had sent a tree. And that another was donating ice cream. And that there were going to be presents. But the Littlest Orphan did not even smile. His wan face was set and drawn. Dire punishment waited him after his hurts were healed. And there would be no Christ Baby to go to for comfort and cheer when the punishment was over.

The morning dragged on. Miss Mace brought his luncheon of bread and milk and was as kind to him as she dared to be—your Miss Maces have been made timorous by a too forceful world. Once, during the early afternoon, the Matron came in to examine his bruised head, and once a maid came to rub the colored stains from the hearth. The Littlest Orphan caught his breath as he watched her.

And then it began to grow dark, and the children were brought upstairs to be washed and dressed in clean blouses for the entertainment. They had been warned not to talk with him, and they obeyed—for there were folk watching and listening. But even so, flickers of conversation—excited, small-boy conversation—drifted to the Littlest Orphan's waiting ears.

Someone had said there was to be a Santa Claus. In a red suit and a white beard. Perhaps . . . it was true. The Littlest Orphan slid down under the covers and pulled the sheet high over his aching head. He didn't want the rest to know that he was crying.

The face-washing was accomplished swiftly. Just as swiftly were the blouses adjusted to the last tie, string, and button. And then the children filed downstairs, and the Littlest Orphan was left alone again. He pulled himself up gingerly until he sat erect, and buried his face in his hands.

Suddenly, from downstairs, came the sound of music. First, the tiny piano, and then the voices of the children as they sang. Automatically the Littlest Orphan joined in, his voice quavering weakly through the empty place. He didn't want to sing—there was neither rhythm nor melody in his heart. But he had been taught to sing those songs, and sing them he must.

First, there was "O Little Town of Bethlehem." And then a carol. And then the one about "Gold and frank-in-sense and myrrh." Strange that the words did not mean flowers tonight! And then there was a hush—perhaps it was a prayer. And then a burst of clapping and a jumble of glad cries. Perhaps that was the Santa Claus in his trappings of white and scarlet. The Littlest Orphan's tears came like hot rain to his tired eyes.

There was a sound in the hall. A rubber-heeled step on the bare floor. The Littlest Orphan slid down again under the covers, until only the bandage on the brow was at all visible. When the Matron stooped over him, she could not even glimpse his eyes. With a vigorous hand she jerked aside the covers.

"Sick or not," she told him, "you've got to come downstairs. Mrs. Benchly wants to see the boy who broke her son's memorial picture. I'll help you with your clothes."

Trembling violently, the Littlest Orphan allowed himself to be wedged into undies and a blouse and a pair of coarse, dark trousers. He laced his shoes with fingers that shook with mingled fear and weakness. And then he

followed the Matron out of the dormitory and through the long halls, with their mocking festoons of red and green crepe paper, and into the assembly room where the lights were blinding and the Christmas tree was a blaze of glory.

The trustees sat at one end of the room, the far end. There was a mass of dark colors, blacks and browns and somber grays. Following in the wake of the Matron, the Littlest Orphan stumbled toward them. Mrs. Benchly—would she beat him in front of all the rest? Would she leap at him accusingly from that dark mass? He felt smaller than he had ever felt before, and more inadequate.

The children were beginning to sing again. But despite their singing, the Matron spoke. Not loudly, as she did to the children, but with a curious deference.

"This is John, Mrs. Benchly," she said, "the child who broke the picture."

Biting his lips, so that he would not cry out, the Littlest Orphan stood in the vast shadow of the Matron. He shut his eyes. Perhaps if this Mrs. Benchly meant to strike him, it would be best to have his eyes shut. And then suddenly a voice came, a voice so soft that somehow he could almost feel the velvet texture of it.

"Poor child," said the voice. "He's frightened. And ill, too. Come here, John. I won't hurt you, dear."

Opening his eyes incredulously, the Littlest Orphan stared past the Matron into the sort of face small children dream about. Violet-eyed and tender. Lined, perhaps, and sad about the mouth, and wistful. But so sweet! Graying hair, with a bit of wave in it, brushed back from a broad, white brow. And slim, white, reaching hands. The Littlest Orphan went forward without hesitation. Something about

this lady was reminiscent of the Christ Baby. As her white hand touched his, tightened on it, he looked up into her face with the ghost of a smile.

The children had crowded almost informally to the other end of the room, toward the tree. The dark mass of the trustees was dissolving, breaking up into fragments that followed the children. One of the trustees laughed aloud. Not at all like an ogre. A sudden sense of gladness began, for no understandable reason, to steal across the Littlest Orphan's consciousness. Rudely the voice of the Matron broke in upon it.

"I have warned the children," she said, "not to disturb anything. Last evening, before they retired, John deliberately disobeyed. And the picture is ruined in consequence. What do you think we had better do about it, Mrs. Benchly?"

* * * * *

For a moment the lady with the dream face did not speak. She was drawing the Littlest Orphan nearer, until he touched the satin folds of her black gown, and despite the Matron's voice, he was not afraid. When at last she answered the Matron, he did not flinch.

"I think," she said gently, "that I'll ask you to leave us. I would like to talk with John—alone."

As the Matron walked stiffly away, down the length of the room, Mrs. Benchly lifted the Littlest Orphan onto her lap.

"I know," she said, and her voice was even gentler than it had been, "that you didn't mean to break the picture. Did you, dear?"

41

Eagerly the Littlest Orphan answered, "Oh, no—ma'am!" he told her. "I didn't mean t' break th' Christ Baby."

The woman's arms were about him. They tightened suddenly. "You're so young," she said; "you're such a mite of a thing. I doubt if you could understand why l had the picture made, why I gave it to the home here, to be hung in the dormitory. My little son was all I had after my husband died. And his nursery—it was such a pretty room—had a Christ Child picture on the wall. And my boy always loved the picture . . . And so when he—left—" Her voice faltered. "I had an artist copy it. I—I couldn't part with the original! And I sent it to a place where there would be many small boys, who could enjoy it as my son had always—" Her voice broke.

The Littlest Orphan stared in surprise at the lady's face. Her violet eyes were misted like April blossoms with the dew upon them. Her lips quivered. Could it be that she, too, was lonesome and afraid? His hand crept up until it touched her soft cheek.

"I *loved* th' Christ Baby," he said simply.

The lady looked at him. With an effort she downed the quaver in her voice. "I can't believe," she said at last, "that you destroyed the picture purposely. No matter what she"—her glance rested upon the Matron's stiff figure, half a room away—"may think! John, dear, did you mean to spoil the gift I gave—in my small boy's name? Oh, I'm sure you didn't."

All day long the Littlest Orphan had lived in fear and agony of soul. All day long he had known pain, physical pain and the pain of suspense. Suddenly he buried his face in the lady's neck—he had never known before that there

was a place in ladies' necks just made for tiny heads—and the tears came. Choked by sobs, he spoke.

"No'm," he sobbed, "I didn't mean to . . . It was only because I was cold. And lonesome. And th' bed was—big. An' all th' rest was asleep. An' the Christ Baby always looked so pink . . . an' glad . . . an' warm. An' I wanted t' take him inter my bed an' cuddle close!" He burrowed his head deeper into the neck—"so that I wouldn't be cold anymore. Or lonesome—anymore."

The lady's arms tightened about the Littlest Orphan's body until the pressure almost hurt, but it was a nice sort of hurt. It shocked her, somehow, to feel the thinness of that body. And her tears fell quite unrestrained upon the Littlest Orphan's bandaged head. And then all at once she bent over. And her lips pressed, ever so tenderly, upon the place where his cheek almost met her ear.

"Not to be cold," she whispered, more to herself than to the Littlest Orphan, "or lonesome anymore! To have the nursery opened again—and the sound of the tiny feet in the empty rooms. To have the Christ Child smiling down upon a sleeping little boy. To kiss bruises away again . . . Not to be lonesome anymore, or cold—"

Suddenly she tilted back the Littlest Orphan's head, was looking deep, deep into his bewildered eyes.

"John," she said, and his name sounded so different when she said it, "how would you like to come away from here, and live in my house, with me? How would you like to be my boy?"

A silence had crept over the other end of the room. One of the trustees, who wore a clerical collar, had mounted the platform. He was reading from the Bible that visiting

ministers read from of a Sunday. His voice rang, resonant and rich as an organ tone, through the room.

"For unto us a child is born," he read, "*unto us a son is given.*"

The Littlest Orphan, with a sigh of utter happiness, crowded closer into the arms that held him.

And it was Christmas Eve!

Rebecca's Only Way

Annie Hamilton Donnell

Christmas in My Heart 3 stood out for a number of reasons: the publisher had run out of Christmassy woodcut illustrations, and we had run through our best Christmas stories. If the series were to continue beyond two books, Connie and I would be forced to go on a buying spree for stories and illustrations that would continue down through the years, as long as Christmas-aholics continued to buy them each year. So, after we prayerfully explored our options, we concluded that God was calling us to a special ministry of Christmas stories, a ministry that might radically change the course of our lives.

So, each time you pull that red Christmas in My Heart 3 off your shelves, remember that this collection was the pivotal one, made possible by our crossing the Rubicon, investing major resources in keeping the series alive year after year. It was a stellar collection of luminaries such as Temple Bailey, Howard C. Schade, William J. Lederer, Annie Hamilton Donnell, Norman Vincent Peale, Bess Streeter Aldrich, Eric P. Kelly, Taylor Caldwell, Hartley F. Dailey, Henry Van Dyke, and Margaret Sangster—no longer would we coast, but rather, we must henceforth search for greatness in each collection.

But what separated our collections from those published elsewhere was our determination to choose only those stories that moved us so deeply they proved to be almost impossible to forget—author name recognition and critical acclaim alone would never be enough. Over time, our readers bought into our unique perspective of choosing stories we strongly felt ought to be preserved for posterity. Readers began to trust my choices.

Annie Hamilton Donnell loved children. In fact, it's hard to find a story bearing her name that does not have children at the heart of it. She never wrote in a sophisticated way; the stories had simple plots, but each line tugged at your heartstrings. Quite a number of her stories featured orphans—including this one in Christmas in My Heart 3. Generations of children have begged their parents, night after night, to "read 'Rebecca's Only Way,' " over and over. I am convinced that Donnell wrote her stories to be read aloud to children. As you read this story, you won't be able to get very far before you realize the powerful impact such stories have on the minds, dreams, aspirations, and character of children who are lucky enough to be exposed to their lines early on.

* * * * *

The thin blue line wound evenly through the corridor and out of the big doors. Just out—no farther. At the first whiff of the blessed freedom of out-of-doors, the line broke into 63 pieces, every "piece" a little free blue orphan. The silence broke, too, into 63 shouts. For an hour the 63 little lone ones would forget that they were lone, and be joyous little players in the sun.

In a corner Rebecca and Sarah Mary had their playhouse; they were "partners."

"I know somethin'!" sang Sarah Mary, bursting with the joy of what she knew, "about Christmas. THERE'S GOIN' TO BE DOLLS! A trustee said it. 'Dolls,' she said, just like that!"

"Oh!" breathed Rebecca. "But I don't suppose she said one APIECE—"

"She did! She said 'every orphan,' an' that's one apiece! An old lady left some money because once SHE wanted a doll an' didn't anybody know it. An' guess who's goin' to dress 'em."

"Oh, I can't wait to guess!"

Sarah Mary edged closer.

"A—live—dressmaker!"

"A live—WHAT?"

There was actual awe in Rebecca's voice.

"Dressmaker—in pieces o' silk an' satin an' TRIMMIN'S!"

Rebecca sat very still. She felt that beautiful Christmas doll warm against her little-mother breast. If she rocked gently—like this—and sang a soft hushaby, her baby would go to sleep! In its silky-satin little dress!

Sarah Mary was chattering on. "I was helpin' Ellen carry the lemonade in for the trustees. Somebody said, 'Sh—little pitchers!' That was me. They were afraid I'd hear, an' I did! The dressmaker is a relation to the person-that-wanted-a-doll-once; and she said—the dressmaker— she'd make the dresses for her part. Don't you hope yours will be sky-blue, Rebecca?"

"Oh, yes, sky-blue!" thrilled Rebecca. *Though red would be lovely, or goldy yellow, or green. If she didn't have ANY color dress, I'd love her,* Rebecca thought, rocking her

darling-to-be in the tender cradle of her arms.

For ten days Rebecca thought of the Christmas doll by day, and dreamed of it by night. A dozen times she named it. Sweet—Love—Delight—Joy—a dozen beauteous names. The tenth day she settled upon Joy. Her little silk child, Joy!

The eleventh day Rebecca saw the picture. It seemed to start up out of all her happy dreamings and dangle before her eyes—"Look! Look at me! Look at my dreadful little orphans!" And Rebecca looked with shocked and horror-stricken eyes. The picture stayed right there, dangling. Nights, too, she could see it. A visitor to the home had brought the paper and read to the children about the hungry orphans across the sea, who were glad for just one meal a day. How contented, then, the visitor had said, ought these orphans at the Saint Luke Home to be with their breakfasts and dinners and suppers!

* * * * *

When she went away, she left the paper; and in it Rebecca saw the picture. A score of thin, sad little faces looked out at her. Such hungry faces! One smiled a little, and the smiling hungry face hurt most.

They are orphans, too; I'm kind of a relation to them, thought Rebecca. "But I'm never hungry. Oh, never!" She could not feel herself that kind of "relation." One night she went without her supper, and lay in the dark on her cot in the row of little cots, trying how it felt to be hungry. If she hadn't had that apple between meals—probably those other orphans never had apples between. Perhaps

if she didn't eat any breakfast tomorrow. But at breakfast Rebecca ate her bowl of cereal eagerly. She could hardly wait for the breakfast bell. It was terrible to be hungry! That night Rebecca dreamed of her Christmas doll, but it was made of bread. A bread child that she rocked in her arms! And a score of sad little children stood round her as she rocked, and the smiling one broke Rebecca's heart, so that—in the dream—she held her Joy-child out to her, and said, "You may eat her—my beautiful child!"

The picture first, and then the plan. Rebecca made that plan with sweating little soul—it was such a bitter, hard plan to make!

There was so little time left. Anxiously she watched her chance, but it was two days before Christmas before it came. She was sent downtown on an errand, and as a special favor given permission to "look in the windows." That meant she need not hurry. She could do her own errands, too.

She was a little scared. It wouldn't be exactly . . . easy. A great automobile stood before a toy shop, and a lady was preparing to alight. She was going in to buy a doll for her little girl! Rebecca read it all instantly, for she was Rebecca.

"Wait! Oh, if you'd only just as LIEVES wait! I—I've got one to sell—I mean a doll for your little girl. With a silk dress that a real live dressmaker made! If you'd just as LIEVES buy mine—"

The small, earnest face gazed upward into the surprised face of the lady. There was no doubting the child's seriousness of purpose, however wild her words sounded. The lady was interested.

"May I see it—the dolly you have to sell?" she said smilingly.

A faint pink color surged into Rebecca's cheeks, and deepened to red.

"I haven't got her yet. You—you'll have to trust me to deliver her Christmas. If you'd only as LIEVES trust me!" cried Rebecca.

"My dear! Suppose you come up here into the car, and sit down beside me, and tell me all about it."

"Yes'm—oh, yes'm, I will. It won't start, will it, while I'm getting in? I never was in one before."

On the broad, soft seat Rebecca drew a long breath. Then quite simply she explained the plan.

"So I've got to get some money to buy bread," she concluded wistfully. "Do you think a doll would buy quite a lot? A SILK doll that a dressmaker dressed? If—if you was going to buy your little girl a silk doll, would you think a dollar'd be a great deal to pay?" Oh, a dollar was a great deal! But a great deal of bread was needed. And bread had gone up; the matron said so. Rebecca set her lips firmly.

"I've got to ask a great deal for my chi—I mean, doll. An' I'm going to sell my orange an' stockin' o' candy, too; we always have those at Saint Luke's Christmas."

The lady's eyes, gazing backward through the years, were seeing the crumpled pink face of the little girl who had not lived long enough for dolls or Christmas candles. "My dear," the lady said gently, "I will buy your dolly. Here is the dollar. Now shall I drive you to Saint Luke's? You are from Saint Luke's Orphanage, aren't you?"

"Yes'm, I'm a Saint Luke orphan, an' I'd like to be driven, thank you, but I've got two places to stop at first."

"We will stop; tell us where. You may start now, James."

To Rebecca, the "Saint Luke orphan," that ride was a thrilling adventure, so thrilling that she forgot her two stopping places entirely; and the big car had to turn about and retrace its swift, glorious way.

"Are you afraid? Shall I ask James to go slower?"

"Oh, don't! Oh, I mean, please don't ask James!"

Rebecca's cheeks were scarlet, her eyes like stars. "I love to fly this way!" Rebecca craned an eager neck, and shouted to the lady above the whir of the car and her whirring little heart, "Do you—s'pose—James—would drive clear—up?"

"Clear up?"

"Yes'm—to Saint Luke's door, so they could see me, 'specially Sarah Mary. If James would just as lieves—"

"James would 'just as lieves,' " the lady said with a smile.

* * * * *

The fruitman's was the first stop. Rebecca stepped down carefully, and stated her amazing errand to him with perfect simplicity.

"Will you buy an orange?" she said clearly. "It will be a nice orange, I think. I'll deliver it Christmas morning, but if you'd just as lieves pay for it now—"

Over Rebecca's head the foreigner's eye caught that of the Lady of the Automobile, and some message appeared to travel to him across the short space—over Rebecca's head. It was as if the Lady of the Automobile said to him, "Buy the orange; I will make it all right." She seemed a rich lady, and the automobile was very grand and big—and the risk was very small.

"If it is not too much a price," the man said gravely.

"Oh! Oh, just a—a loaf of bread!" Rebecca stammered nervously. "Could you pay as much as that? I need the bread—I mean THEY need—"

Was the Lady of the Automobile holding up ten fingers? The man went into his little store, and came back. Into Rebecca's hand he dropped two nickels. And Rebecca never knew that the lady dropped two into his.

"He was a nice fruitman," Rebecca said, and added shyly: "an' you were very nice. I'm glad everybody's nice—I kind of dreaded it. I never expected to have a beautiful time!" She jingled her money joyously. "It must be quite a lot o' bread, it makes so much noise!" she laughed.

At a candy store the lady accompanied Rebecca. Once more a message flashed silently over the child's head. The remarkable advance sale of a Christmas "stockin' o' candy" was accomplished without difficulty.

"Why, so was SHE nice! Now I can take the money to the orphans," Rebecca cried. "I know the way; that visitor told us."

And to the whimsical fancy of the lady it would hardly have been unexpected if Rebecca had gravely asked if James would just as lieves take her overseas to lay this unique gift of bread before the hungry children themselves.

"I'm glad it will buy a lot of bread; they're very hungry orphans. One of them is smiling—I couldn't SMILE, could you? But perhaps the orphans over the sea are courageouser. Than Saint Luke orphans, I mean. I couldn't hardly WAIT for my breakfast—" Rebecca broke off at that shameful little memory. Oh, these other orphans had to wait!

At the Relief Headquarters Rebecca went in alone. She did not talk much to her new acquaintance the rest of the way back to the Saint Luke Orphanage. And she had forgotten her desire to show off to Sarah Mary. It had come suddenly to Rebecca that it was her dear child Joy she had left behind her. A great anguish grew within her—the anguish of affection. Her JOY was dead.

The matron of Saint Luke's had always maintained that Rebecca Dill was a very DIFFERENT orphan from the rest. The queer notions that child took! And now this notion to have her Christmas doll—how did she know there was going to be one?—tied up tight in a paper bag—

"If you'd just as lieves," Rebecca pleaded. "I don't want to see her. I mean it would be EASIER. With a string tied 'round the top."

* * * * *

But Rebecca was not to be present at the Christmas Eve celebration at the Saint Luke Orphanage. She was feverish and so nearly sick that the matron decided she must stay in bed. It was Sarah Mary who carried her up the doll (her beautiful, darling child!) in the paper bag, and the candy and the orange. It was to Sarah Mary that Rebecca entrusted the delicate mission of "delivering" them all the next morning to their separate owners.

"Aren't you goin' to LOOK at it, Rebecca Dill? Not PEEK?" It was all very puzzling and unheard of to Sarah Mary. "Mine slept with me last night, right in my bed. I

could hear her silk dress creakin' in the dark."

"Mine creaked, too," whispered Rebecca, though of course it might have been the paper bag. "She slept with me, an' I kissed her through a little teeny hole." Rebecca did not say that she had poured her anguished, torn young soul through that "teeny" hole—that she had cried: "Oh, my beloved little child, how can I let you go? Oh, my sweetest, never forget your mother loved you!"

On Christmas afternoon came the Automobile Lady to Saint Luke's. She was a flushed and starry-eyed lady. In her hand she had a curious paper bag, tied at the top. Would the matron send it up to the little Rebecca-orphan, who, it seemed, was sick? Surely not very sick—

"A little feverish, that's all; children often are," the matron said. And the lady smiled gratefully at the reassurance.

"I can go and see her?" she asked. "Not just yet—in a few minutes."

Up in her bed Rebecca tremblingly opened the paper bag. But first she read a "teeny" dangling note.

"The dolly I bought for my little girl—will my little girl love it as I am going to love her?

THE AUTOMOBILE LADY."

And under the signature Rebecca found a tiny postscript—oh, a beautiful, dear postscript!

"If you'd just as lieves be my little girl—"

Pink Angel

Author Unknown

Christmas in My Heart 4 (the first blue cover) came out in 1995. All too often, I find it impossible to track down an author or original source for a story. Many times, readers help me track them down. One of these, "Pink Angel," we anthologized in '95. Unfortunately, even after all this time, we still have been unable to identify this author. In it, a significant truth is explored: Mothers are entrusted with one of God's greatest gifts to our world: validating each child's sense of self-worth—almost impossible for a human being to succeed without it.

* * * * *

There's always a special minute when it comes. Every year. Christmas, I mean.

Sometimes it's when the tree is up and trimmed and you step back from it and see it sparkle for the first time and hear it tinkling a little. And you smell that smell—of a piece of the woods brought indoors.

Sometimes it's a time when you find just the right present for someone you're very fond of and you bring it home and work over the wrapping. Or you get some special thing you never dreamed you would. Like that time I was emptying my stocking, and I saw the box underneath it move and the cover push up and two green eyes looked out and it was Magnolia, the black kitten. That was the minute that year. Often it's a song—on the radio or in church or once even the garbage man singing "Joy to the World" while he banged frozen-in grapefruit peels out of our can.

But it's always a minute that's special, and then Christmas is there. It's come for you. It hits you and leaves bells ringing in your ears.

It came twice for me that year. The first time was on a Thursday, and we had only the next week and a half to go before vacation.

I had been feeling low ever since after Thanksgiving when they gave out the parts for the Christmas program. My brother Pud came home all hepped up over getting a speaking part in his school play. My little brother Bumps was going to be one of the three kings of Orient. Even my tiny sister—she was going to be an angel in the Benjamin School play. Four rooms in her school and a little five-year-old kid gets a solo part! I'm the dumb one. The big brother in junior high, that's me. I get nothing.

Mother glowed when they told her. That's a nice thing about Mother. If you do something good, you sure get appreciation.

"Just think!" she said. "Such smart children I have. Some people have *one* smart one, one that gets into things. Look at me. Every single one. Jean, singing a whole verse of 'Away in a Manger' all by herself. King Balthazar Bumps, Innkeeper Pud." She looked at me. "And Rod," she said.

I laughed. "Yeah," I said, "and Rod."

"Well," Mother said, "playing in the orchestra isn't to be sneezed at. Playing a trumpet in an orchestra is fully as important as anything else," she said. But she swelled her voice too much on it. She was feeling sorry for me. She was proud of the others. She was sorry for me.

So it was her face lighting up that I saw on Thursday when Miss Phelps told me. Even before I got home, before I ever told her, that's what I could see. Mother's face glowing with pride. Christmas had come. Only this time it didn't last.

It began to snow on the way home, and that made everything perfect. I ran the last block. I would have flown if I could fly. Snow for Christmas and me with the lead in the Christmas play! I couldn't wait to tell it. I wouldn't wait. Would Mother's eyes shine! It was too bad about Jim having to go to California, but *me*!

I stood for a minute by the door, watching the snow, catching flakes on my tongue, trying to get myself quiet before I went in. I didn't want Mother to think I cared so much. I wanted to sound like it wasn't so much, me getting the lead.

I'd have to get a shepherd costume, a sheepskin thing they wanted, but Mother would do that. She was good at things like that.

"We must have a sheepskin someplace," she'd say, "under some of this junk around here," she'd say and her eyes would be shining at me, hardly believing it. . . . She'd pooh-pooh the costume. "I'll get one," she'd say. "My goodness, for the boy with the biggest part in the play, we'll find a costume. We'll *buy* a sheep and *skin* it if we have to," she'd say. "Just you leave it to me."

I took a big gulp of the Christmas air and went in. "Our program's Wednesday afternoon," I said. Just casual. Nobody knew I was the star.

"Wednesday," Mother said. "That's the twenty-first," She was piling cookies into a can. "Here, take one," she said.

It crumbled when I bit it. Pecans inside.

A lock of hair was in Mother's eyes, and she pushed it away with her arm. She looked tired. She said, "Rod, can you come right home after school and stay with Jean?"

"Yeah, I guess so," I said. "Unless we have to practice." I took a big breath. "You see," I said, trying not to act excited, "I—"

"That's good," Mother said. "I've simply got to go downtown. There's Mable and Lucile I haven't even looked for presents for yet. And Jeanie's presents for the neighborhood children. I'll have to take her along for that. And I haven't any of the family presents yet."

"I have a lot to do, Mother," I said.

"I know," Mother said. "Everybody's busy. It's getting so that's all there is to Christmas anymore. Rush, rush, rush. I hope Father can address cards tonight. He just has to take that over. When you come home, Rod, stop in at Rich's and see if you can get a box that would fit that stuff." She nodded to a chair full of packages in the corner. "I have to get that stuff off right away, or it'll never get there for Christmas. Just think! Only two weeks away. It drives me crazy when I think of it."

About a week for me. A week to learn that part! It kinda drove me crazy too.

"Mother," I said, "I need a lot of time myself for—" but she was putting the can of cookies out on the back porch and talking.

"But not this noon," she was saying. "There's salad in the refrigerator. Get it out, will you?" She came back in and started putting dishes on the table. "We don't really have time to eat anymore," she said. "Where are Bumps and Pud anyway? Look out the window, Rod, and see what's keeping them. Jean, get your bib on and start eating. I should start you at eleven-thirty, the way you dawdle."

I gave up trying to tell her then. A thing like that you can't blurt out. I called my brothers.

They came in and dropped their jackets, and Bumps said, "I'll have to have that king of Orient's costume, you know."

Mother sighed and dried her hands on the towel by the sink. "Butter a roll for Jean, Rod," she said. "What do kings of Orient wear? Bright colors, mostly, I guess. I'll look in the trunk. I know!" she said then. "Maybe I can borrow that bright blue flannel peignoir of Barbara's and work it from there."

"What's a peignoir?" Bumps said. "I'm not going to wear girl's clothes!"

"It's a robe," Mother said. "Kings have to wear robes. Don't worry. I'll figure out something real kingly. I always do, don't I? Why couldn't you have been one of the singers—in everyday clothes? Why did you all have to be so talented, you smart children you!" She grinned. "Making so much work! I have to think up king's costumes while I'm pushing through crowds looking for some nice little thing for the woman who was so nice to us last summer."

My, she didn't have time to listen to me tell about getting the lead, much less find a costume for me! You couldn't help being sorry Mother was so busy she had to eat on the run. But it made you kind of mad too. That she had to be so busy when you had such an important thing to tell. So

busy she couldn't stop long enough to hear. My—this was big stuff! This was big. Not just a verse of a song. Not just a speaking part, not just a king of Orient. This was the *lead*.

"You didn't have to send that woman up north a present," I said. "You didn't have to."

"Well, I want to," Mother said. "But it's that angel costume for Jean which has me whirling right this minute. Angel costume, indeed. They're balmy over at that school."

Jean's lip shook a little, and she pushed a piece of pear around with her fork. Mother was pouring hot water over her tea bag in her cup. She put the kettle back on the stove quick and patted Jean's shoulder.

"Oh, don't worry, darling. I'll do 'er," Mother said. "I'll do 'er up brown."

"Not brown," said Jean unsteadily. "Pink."

"Yeah, pink," Mother said. "You'll be the angelest angel in town. Just you push some salad into that angel mouth."

Jean's eyes were shining wet, and she ate a big bite of salad.

"I know my part," she said. Her eyes were almost dancing out of her head! For Jean it was now. It was the first time. As long as I live I'll never forget that first time for me in kindergarten. The Magic Star-maker, that was me. I remembered, looking at Jean, how wonderful I felt when I came home and told it; how it was, that day. A sea of faces with clapping hands beneath them. And Mother in the second row. That's the way it would be for Jean. The Christmas tree would sparkle in the corner, the people would smell wintery and Christmasy, the excitement would be racing all around, and she'd be good and Mother would be watching! Oh, it's always wonderful, but the first time it's magic.

"I know it perfect," Jean said. "Want to hear it?"

"Darling, I can't hear it too often," Mother said, and Jean dropped her fork and stood on her chair and sang it, bobbing her head with the rhythm of it, her long blond hair bouncing, her eyes big and dark and serious.

"The cat-tle are low-ing the poor baby wakes
But lit-tle Lord Je-sus, no cry-ing He makes.
I love Thee, Lord Je-sus, look down from the sky
And stay by my cra-dle till morning is nigh."

Sure hits the down beat, Jean does.

"Oh, it's so wunnerful," she said. "Wasn't I lucky to get pink for my angel suit, Mother? They pulled the colors out of a box, and Alice got blue and Gail got white and pink was left for me and that's best." I guess we'd heard about it a hundred times, but Jean was still telling it with gusto. Mother was listening with gusto, too, her face beaming at Jean.

So I decided to wait. I decided not to tell Mother my big news till later, till she wasn't so busy that having to find a shepherd costume would be the last straw. I'd wait till I was alone with her so I could have all that gloating for me alone.

Mother gathered up her dishes and put them in the sink and sat Jean down again. She kissed the top of her head. "Eat the lettuce," she said. "You're going to have an angel suit that'll knock their eyes out. You know what I found this morning? An old pink formal I had once. You're going to be a stiff little pink tulle angel, darling. Finish eating and I'll show you. Tonight we'll cut it out. It isn't the gown

that worries me, it's those wings. But we'll figure it out. Do you know your part, Bumps?"

Did he know his part? Wait'll she heard about me. The whole lead to learn in a week.

"Sure," Bumps said. "I just walk. Step and hold, step and hold. It's easy. You got something for the murr?"

"The murr?" Mother said.

"Yeah," said Bumps. "You know, 'Murr is mine its bitter perfume breathes a life of gathering bloom sawring sighing bleeding dying sealed in a stone-cold tomb oh oh!' "

"Oh, myrrh," Mother said. "No, I haven't. But I'll look around. Goodness, you make it mournful. Don't you know how to sing it?"

"I don't sing it," Bumps said. "I just march it."

"What?" Mother said, surprised. "I thought it was your rich voice you were picked for, but you just march it? It was your gorgeous physique and kingly carriage you got chosen for—well, well. And your costume—resourceful Mother, perhaps. Pud, you stop at Benson's shop for sure and get

that cloak you're going to wear so I can wash it tonight. Oh, Rod, you are a comfort to me! I like people whose talents run to playing trumpets in school orchestras in plain suits of clothes."

"Well,"—it wasn't exactly a good opening for it, but: "Mother, I'm not going to play in the orchestra," I said.

"Oh," Mother said. A sharp little oh. "That's too bad," she said. "But don't you care, Rod. It's fun just to sit and watch. We have to have watchers too. We have to have an audience or there couldn't be any programs."

"Well, I'm not going to—" I began, but just then Jean stood up and handed her plate across to Mother.

"See, I cleaned it up," she said. "I better practice my part again, Mother."

"Oh, you know that thing frontwards and backwards," Bumps said.

"I do not," Jean said. "We have to march too. We have to march up when they play the piano. You can't go too fast. 'The cat-tle are low-ing the poor baby wakes—' "

Suddenly I saw red. What if she was little, what if I was the oldest? Mother was my Mother too. Why couldn't I even have a chance to tell her about me?

"Oh, keep still a minute!" I said. "Mother! I'm not going to watch!"

"Rod!" Mother said. "Let her practice her part! My goodness, it takes practice to march and sing like an angel." And then she lowered her voice. "She's little, darling, let her enjoy it. Remember how it is the first time."

"Sure," I said. I could wait. My news would blow her over when it came. I could wait.

I worked on it while I was staying with Jean. And by

dinnertime I just about knew it. Mother came home with Father, both of them loaded with packages, Mother's face sagging with tiredness. She sank into a chair and kicked off her shoes and closed her eyes.

"Poor Father," she said. "If I had to battle that streetcar gang every night, I'd give up. Get my slippers, Pud. Get Father's slippers."

"It's not quite that bad all the time," Father said.

"I'd like to fall into bed," Mother said, "without undressing. Thank goodness for automatic ovens anyway. We come home, open the magic door and there it is—meat loaf and scalloped potatoes. All we have to do is set the table."

"That's wonderful," Father said. "I'll have to learn that trick. What number do you set it at to get turkey?"

"There's a little more to it than that," Mother said. "But I do have one trick I'm going to need you for tonight. I'll show you how. All you have to do is sit in the chair by the desk and put a pen between your thumb and forefinger and turn your back to us. There's a list and a pile of envelopes and in about three hours' time, presto—addressed Christmas cards all ready to go!"

I stacked the dishes and went to my room to study. I studied my part. As soon as the kids went to bed I'd tell her. And when I told her, I'd know it. She could hold the book while I'd say it over. Nothing nice and average about me. I get a lead in the morning, by night I know it. I was doing it in front of the mirror without the book when I heard her call.

"Everyone!" she called. "Hey, come and look. Just come and look!"

Pud ran down ahead of me, and Bumps came banging out of the bathroom. Father had come from the study and stood with his pen in his hand. Mother was in the middle of the floor, and there were pink threads and scissors and pins in a box and over at the far end of the living room was Jean.

My breath stopped. And for a second it was all pure Christmas—something you can't quite keep but only can remember a little. There was Jean, a fluffy pink glittering angel, too beautiful to believe. It went straight from the neck, the gown, clear down to her ankles, and her arms were lost in it and it was like pink foam, like glistening spun sugar, ready to disappear; and floating above it, with sparkling wings just showing in back, Jeanie's wide-eyed face. I never knew she was that pretty. All creamy pink and her mouth a little open and her eyes round and big and dark and her hair a soft golden crown around her head.

"My, that's pretty!" Bumps said.

And Pud said, "Wowie!"

And Father said, "Oh Honey, don't look so beautiful or someone's going to steal you away from us!"

And Mother said, "Isn't she darling?"

And Jean put one hand over her mouth and drew in her breath in a little gaspy delighted laugh and wriggled her shoulders, and then Father said, "I'll get the lights, I'll get the camera; we have to have a picture of that!" Father took the picture and then my world went spinning.

"Couldn't they let you off from work, Father?" Jean asked. "Couldn't they let you off for a good program like that? It's gonna be awful good!"

"I don't know but they might," Father said. "I don't know but they'd almost have to. When is this affair?"

"It's two o'clock," Jean said, "but we have to come ahead of time. Two o'clock Wednesday," Jean said.

"Of course, Wednesday. There isn't any school on Thursday, silly." Mother unfastened the angel gown and pulled it up over Jean's head.

"Wednesday?" I said, standing real still. "The twenty-first?" I said.

"Yup," Jean said, pulling her undershirt down over her stomach. "Wednesday, December the twenty-first at two P.M., and everybody better get there early to get a good seat. You better get there early, Mother, and then you can sit right in front."

Mother smiled down at her. "Hurry now," she said. "It's past bedtime for all of you. What's the matter with you, Rod? Don't stand there dreaming. It's late."

I followed them upstairs. I went to my room and closed the door. I put the copy of the play in the drawer of my desk and locked the drawer. It was a long time before I could get to sleep.

We practiced every morning before school. We practiced every day during school. We practiced sometimes after school. By the end of the next week I knew it frontwards and backwards. I knew it sideways. I knew the leading part of the play in less than a week with nobody helping me. I knew it, but it wasn't any good. Nobody was going to see me. Why should I care? Who cares if I'm any good?

It was the way they had schools in our town. All of us in different schools, that was why. They didn't plan it for

I'd think about how it would be if I was to say, "Hey, Mom, I've got the lead in our Christmas play. I've got the lead, Mom." I don't know how it would have come out. I don't know what Mother could have done about it. If she came to see me it would break Jeanie's heart. I knew that. If she didn't come—it was better for Mother not to know about it at all than to have to know and not come. I kept still.

So on Monday Miss Phelps says I'm no good. "I thought you were better than Jim had been," she said. "You read it so well that first day. What's happened to you? Please try harder," she said. "Try to think how you'd feel if you were that shepherd boy who had to stay behind when the others went to Bethlehem. You're the one that's left out, the one that nothing big can happen to. Try to make it feel like that."

"OK," I said. What did they expect of a just—average kid? What did they expect?

"And you'll have to have that costume by tomorrow," she said.

"OK," I said.

I didn't care what I wore. I went up in the attic at noon and looked in the trunk. So, who cared what the shepherd boy wore? Who cared anyway? Sheepskin. What did they think? That people just had sheepskin lying around their houses?

There wasn't anything in the trunk. Satin dresses, striped pants, silk scarves. I bundled the junk all up and rammed it back in and closed the lid. It was cold up there in the attic but I didn't care. I dropped down on the rug in front of the trunk and put my head on my arm, face down. Maybe I'd catch cold so I couldn't be in the play. I didn't

people who had more than one child. Jean went to Benjamin. Me, I went to junior high. What did they care about people who had kids in Benjamin and West Side? People weren't supposed to have kids a lot of different ages. What did they care if the programs came the same day, the same hour? What was that to them?

I couldn't even tell her about the costume. I didn't know what to do about that. Maybe I was a softy, but I couldn't do that to Jean. I'd look at her at mealtime, jabbering away about their program, jabbery-happy, and I'd think about it.

care. Christmas sure was a lot of bother and work. That's the way it is, I guess, when you grow up. I was getting old, was all. It's kind of tough, outgrowing Christmas.

Can't blame a kid for crying when he gets that blue. I felt better after a while. I sat up and wiped my eyes on my sweater and waited a few minutes before I went down so my eyes wouldn't be red. Mother thought I was hiding Christmas presents or something up there. It sure was cold. I couldn't find a shepherd costume and I didn't care. Maybe they'd take the part away from me. I shrugged my shoulders and put the rug up around my legs to keep them warm.

It was an old fur rug made from the hide of a cow or something, that Grandpa got once. I stood up and picked up the rug—it was just the thing! All I needed was a hole for my head. I took it down to my room and cut one and tried it on. It looked kind of sad after all, but I sneaked it out to school anyway. It sort of covered me up at least.

The teacher fastened it together at the sides and between the legs with staples. "Guess it'll have to do," she said. "It certainly doesn't look like a sheepskin, though." She sure looked worried. What was so important? Nobody was going to see it.

"Sometimes sheep are black," I said.

"Yes, I know," Miss Phelps said. "But this is brown—or red. Are you sure it was a cow? It has such long hair. And sheep are curly."

"Maybe it's a buffalo from the Western prairies," I said.

"If it was a buffalo," she said, "it must have died of old age. Well, cow or buffalo, it'll just have to do. You aren't supposed to look glamorous after all."

I certainly didn't. I sort of looked like an old buffalo getting ready to die with its hide getting too loose for its frame. I felt like one too.

We got the Christmas tree up that night, and I could almost feel happy again, just looking at it. Every reddish-pink ball made me think of Jean in the angel costume. I was sure glad I hadn't spoiled it for Jean. After all, Christmas is for kids.

On Tuesday, Mother went to the West Side to see Bumps march the king of Orient and carry the myrrh in an old Chinese brass pot she'd borrowed and to hear Pud say his two lines. "They were wonderful," she told Father that night. "Just wonderful! Aren't we lucky to have such gifted children?" she said. "Bumps was kingly and steady and—inspired looking. I was proud of him."

Bumps beamed. "It sure was hard to walk that slow," he said.

"I'll bet," Mother said. "And Pud was wonderful! You'd have thought he really owned that inn. You were wonderful, Pud."

"That's what everybody said," said Pud.

"And now tomorrow is Jean," she said. "My goodness, what would I do if I had eight children? I couldn't take it, I'd be so worn out running from one program to another." Suddenly Mother stopped talking. "Rod!" she said. "I forgot. Oh, Rod! I forgot all about you. Have I missed it? What day is your program? I completely forgot."

"That's OK," I said. "It's tomorrow. You can't go to both."

"Oh, Rod," Mother said. "I did so want to hear you play in the orchestra. Oh, what am I going to do?" You should have seen Jean—she looked like the end of the world.

"Well, you have to go and see Jean," I said, and it was

worth it seeing her come alive again. "Anyway," I said, "I'm not going to play in that old orchestra."

Mother sank back in her chair. "I don't know, Rod," she said. "You always do things right somehow. Every mother ought to have a child like you. You never complicate things; you never foul things up. You always make things come out right, and I love you. You'll play in the orchestra for the spring concert, I know you will; and we'll all go to hear you. Wouldn't you like to stay out and come and see Jean be an angel? I'll write you an excuse. Why don't you?"

"I'd better go to ours," I said simply.

"That's right," Mother said. "That's right. You had better. We wouldn't want anyone to think you were jealous or anything because you didn't get chosen to play with the orchestra this time."

Rod, you always do things right somehow. I kept thinking about Mother saying that, when I was getting my cow skin on.

The teacher was extra-excited. "Please do your best," she said to me. "Do it the way you did that first day, the day you read it. Make it good, Rod," she said, "and then maybe they won't notice your costume. I wonder if it would help any to trim off some of that hair." So she tried it. It gave it more of a French poodle look, and Miss Phelps looked sad and said pleadingly, "Do your best, Rod, please."

OK, I will, I thought. *I'm the one that always does things right somehow.*

It wasn't hard, I'll say that. It wasn't hard to act it. It was just the way I felt. I just acted me, the way I felt upstairs there in the attic the day I found the cow skin. I was getting too old for Christmas. That was for kids. I

was left behind now. Left behind while Jean and Bumps and Pud went ahead and had Christmas. Left behind while the others went to Bethlehem to see the Baby King in the manger. I was the shepherd boy who'd had to get his own costume, who was left behind to tend the sheep so the others could go. My, it wasn't hard at all.

I even got weepy over it. Nobody wants to be left behind while others go on and see the miracle. Nobody wants to grow up, I guess, and take responsibilities, give up things so others can have them. It wasn't hard and I was doing it! I was doing it like a breeze. I threw myself into it, moth-eaten old cow skin and all. And I knew I was good.

I could see Miss Phelps in the wings. Poor Miss Phelps. I'd sure let her down until now. Her face looked droopy and ready to cry. Miss Phelps was dead on her feet, she was too tired and nervous. She'd had to wait through all the orchestra playing, through all the carol singing, nervous because I was such a flop. Now she could hardly believe it. I was good.

I felt sorry for Miss Phelps. She was like me. Nobody cared enough to help her. Until now, I hadn't seen her side of it. Well, I was grown up now. I had to think about those things. It was a sad thing to miss out on Christmas, but you didn't need to spoil it for others.

Only I'd had that little cry when nobody was looking. Up in the attic on the cow skin. And I could cry here in the pasture after the others had gone and I knew I had missed out. I pillowed my head on my arm in the grass of the stage pasture and cried. It came easy. The rest might not be so easy, but the crying was. Next came the hard part. In a minute I'd hear the quartet singing softly up in the rafters: "Peace on earth—" and then would come the hard part. Then I'd have to raise my head in wonder and let it show in my face.

Out of the dusky background on a raised place, lights would come up on the nativity scene. The shepherd boy would see it after all, and I'd have to show how wonderful he felt about it. I hadn't done it right yet. I'd been told often enough. I just couldn't make Nancy and Timmy seem wonderful enough to get all excited over. Not even all dressed up in Bible clothes and leaning over the manger with tableau lights and a fine screen in front of them. Not even with the wonderful animals Perry'd gotten from his father's market. Not even when the shepherds came and the wise men came. Not even in costume. I guess I'm just not made that way. I just kept trying to figure out whose bathrobe they were wearing.

Then I sat up like a shot. Something was goofy. Someone was patting my head! I sat up and turned around and I didn't need to act to look surprised. To look dumbfounded! A glistening pink angel was patting my head, and my mouth dropped open, and I was dumbfounded.

Jean!

And that's when Christmas came the second time. That's when the glory hit me. Hit me with a bang that burst my eardrums, with a blaze that split my eyeballs.

For just one second I looked everywhere because it was too much for me. I just couldn't get it. And afterward they said that was good. As if I was wondering where the music had come from, where the angel had come from.

And I saw Mother!

She was standing in the wings beside Miss Phelps. Was she ever glowing! Maybe she was proud of Jean and Pud and Bumps. She was super-proud of me. Not just because I had the lead. That was small stuff compared to the other. She was proud of me for not spoiling it for Jean. She smiled a wonderful smile, and she motioned with her eyes, and I took Jeanie's hand and turned and looked at the tableau, and if that audience couldn't see the glory shining in my face, they must be blind. It was blinding me.

Sometimes I think that's the peak. I'll probably never again have Christmas hit me like that. Right between the eyes. I hardly heard Mother explaining how Jean's program wasn't very long and she felt badly about me being the left-out one and so she'd gathered her up, wings and all, and had come on over. How they'd told her then, and let them stand in the wings. How wonderful I'd acted, so wonderful that Jean had been taken in and had run to comfort me.

I was still standing there when they all crowded around, squealing and jumping and Miss Phelps crying and telling me our play was going to be put on at the museum—with the sheepskin lining of an old coat of Father's instead of the cow skin, Mother said, and even with Jean. Most people thought it was planned that way, with Jean.

It didn't worry me any. I could do it again. With Mother watching, I could do it easy. I was grown up, I was good, and the bells were ringing in my head.

Maybe Christmas will come again like that some day. But it can never be the same. That will always be the peak—the year I grew up and got hit so hard with the glory of Christmas.

Christmas in Tin Can Valley

Author Unknown

In 1996, we took early retirement, moving from Annapolis, Maryland, to Conifer, Colorado, so that we could keep up with our publishing deadlines.

Occasionally, I am embarrassed because I fail to catch the significance of a given story. Usually, my radar is fairly accurate, and I'll even catch stories that other editors and story anthologists fail to see value in. In Christmas in My Heart 5 is one of these. Year after year after year I'd come across a certain story, but I'd remained immune to its charm and value. I'd devalue it because it seemed so trite and simplistic; it had no real depth to its story line. Finally, one day, an epiphany—yet another reader mailed me a photocopy of the story, giving it high praise. Why hadn't I ever used it? This time I was borderline angry: Not again! So just to get the story off my back, I decided to read it one more time. And . . . you guessed it! This time, I realized what a powerful story it was. I made this poor reject, "Christmas in Tin Can Valley," the lead story, and appreciative letters poured in. It was even made "Christmas Story of the Year" in several venues. And I—I learned a valuable lesson: Don't judge the value of a story by one reading of it.

* * * * *

It was the Yule season in Hollis Hollow, U.S.A. I say U.S.A. because this story could happen in almost any town of our country, yes, even here in this city of ours. Ragged and dirty children, ragged and dirty women, ragged and dirty men, careworn housewives and mothers trying to make their poorly made shacks worthy of the name "home." Discouraged fathers trying to provide for their families on the city's dumping grounds; yes, large cities are familiar with the scene, and it is not uncommon to find, back in the more remote sections of the thriving town or village, places where filth and dirt breed disease, crime, and pathetic conditions.

Tin Can Valley started as a rubbish heap, and not long after the city started using Hollis Hollow as a dumping ground, the poorer element drifted in and gleaned from the rubbish such things that could be used for their physical substance and shelter. Crude shacks were made from store boxes and discarded sheets of tin; old stoves were patched and propped until they were able to give out a little warmth and heat for cooking; discarded bricks and stones were fashioned into crude fireplaces and chimneys; other bits of material, considered useless in more prosperous sections of the city, were eagerly seized by the inhabitants of Tin Can Valley and placed here and there, rigged up with boards, blocks, bricks, and sticks, until various pieces of furniture were peculiarly manufactured out of practically nothing.

Being a resident of Tin Can Valley was nothing of which to be proud, although their names appeared in the papers quite a bit: so many contagious diseases, so many criminal acts, and so many disturbances. But to extend a helping hand, to look upon these people with love as souls

that God wanted in His kingdom, too, wasn't given much thought.

Now the Christmas season was approaching. The stores temptingly displayed their gorgeous merchandise. Eyes grew large, ears opened wide, little minds were active, and imaginations were stretched to the widest possible extent as children, watching and wondering, eagerly anticipated the joys of Christmas morning with that special toy all their own they had gazed at in the shop windows, or on the laden counters, or in the overflowing showrooms. The season was a time of joy for everyone—for everyone, that is, except the people of Tin Can Valley. Little eyes were just as wide, ears could hear just as well, little minds were also active, and imaginations were plentiful, but there was no joy of anticipation. Tired mothers and downhearted fathers had brusquely informed their inquiring youngsters that gifts came only to those who were wealthy, those on the hill, and never, never to Tin Can Valley. Occasionally, some well-meaning church society had sent a basket or two with food and a few discarded toys, but discarded things were so common among the wretched boys and girls that it was nothing to be excited about, nothing like they saw in the brilliantly lighted windows of the business section.

Jimmie lived in Tin Can Valley. His was one of the store box shacks of one room. One small window let in a little light by day, and an oil lamp gave a little light by night—that is, it did when Jimmie could sell a few papers, or his mother could find work as an extra, washing dishes at a nearby restaurant, for money to buy oil with, and then that was bought only after the other necessities were provided for first. Just like any other eight-year-old boy in the Valley, Jimmie was filled with the natural pep and vim of a growing boy.

One day a lady visited the little shack where Jimmie and his widowed mother lived. She smiled so sweetly and spoke so kindly that Jimmie wondered where she had come from. Surely not from the city. His little playmates had told him those people were all cross and mean. Finally he ventured the question "Where did you come from?"

"Not far from here, son," she replied. "I came to help you people here in the Hollow."

"How?" This was something new to Jimmie. No one but Mother had ever offered to help him before.

"First, by telling you a beautiful story," she answered.

Jimmie listened intently. This was so strange, so unreal, so impossible, and yet— *Why, this babe must have been born in a place something like Tin Can Valley,* he decided. But this lady had said that wealthy men brought him pretty gifts because he was a king. After the lady had gone, the boy thought over and over about the words she had spoken, and that night Jimmie crept out under the stars and looked up into the heavens. It was bitterly cold, and he shivered as he drew his coat more closely about his thin body, not noting crunching steps in the crisp snow as he gazed intently heavenward.

"Watcha doin', Jim?" a gruff voice spoke close to his ear as a figure halted near him.

"Lookin' fer the star," he answered.

"Hadn' oughta have any trouble. Plenty of 'em up there," the man replied.

"Not the star that showed where the baby was that

night when Jesus was born," Jimmie answered.

"Better go in an' get warm," the neighbor advised and trudged on to his own little shack, but thinking, *A baby born . . . In a manger . . . Um . . .* Maybe there was something to Christmas after all. He remembered hearing the story when he was a boy, but he had forgotten about the real heart of the story. A pang shot through him as he opened the door. One time he'd had happiness when he knew and believed that story. Perhaps he could find it again.

It was the day before Christmas. The lady again came to see Jimmie and his mother. And this time she invited them both to come to the mission that night. And such wonderful things she promised—lovely music and the Christmas story and gifts, real gifts for each of them! Oh, the joy of anticipation was known to Jimmie now. Jimmie clapped his hands with delight. "But won't you tell me about the baby again right now?" he entreated.

"It is because of Him," she had finished after repeating the story, "that I am here now, and that we are giving you gifts tonight. And He has told us to go and tell others."

Jimmie had never seen anything so wonderful in his whole life. He and his mother sat very near the front. There was such beautiful music, "Joy to the World," and then a man arose and told them softly the story of Jesus. He could hear the soft strains of "O Little Town of Bethlehem." *Why, remember? That was the town where the baby was born!* But the man was speaking again. He was telling the story all over again, only he didn't end with the wise men; he told how the baby grew into a little boy and became a man, and such wonderful things He did helping people, healing them when they were sick, and teaching them how to live. And then—Jimmie's eyes filled with tears—then some cruel men took Him and killed Him. But the man was saying that this Man, whom he called Jesus, had risen from His grave and was, at that very moment, now living in heaven. First dying, and now living so that everyone—*Why,* Jimmie thought, *that means* me!—could live with Him forever more.

Jimmie hung on every word. At last the minister had finished, and some other men were passing out baskets—baskets filled with good things to eat and a toy and candy for every boy and girl in the Valley. It was all so wonderful, and yet Jimmie kept thinking of the story. Quietly, he slipped up to the minister and touched his coat sleeve.

"Say, minister!" he exclaimed. "Did you say that Baby died for people?"

The man looked down with kindly eyes at the upturned face. "Yes, my boy."

"Then He died for me?"

"Yes, sonny."

"And I should tell others who don't know it, shouldn't I? 'Cause the lady said that's why she told me the story."

The man nodded and patted the boy's head.

Then Mother called, and soon Jimmie was nestling up against her in the mission truck as it carried its load back to the Valley.

Tin Can Valley was happier that Christmas Eve than it had ever been before, but Jimmie was happiest of all. There was a newfound peace and joy in his heart that only Christ could give. His heart was filled to overflowing, and he repeated the story over and over to his careworn mother until she too caught a glimpse of the joy offered by the Saviour.

Christmas morning was ushered in by a blustering wind, bearing upon its wings bits of stinging sleet and snow which, as the day lengthened, turned into a blinding blizzard. Jimmie was up at dawn, drawing on his thin coat and worn cap. He kissed his mother and darted out into the snow. At length he returned, cold and shivering. But he was smiling and happy.

"My boy, where have you been?" his mother asked, drawing him toward the little stove that was struggling bravely to radiate a little heat.

"Telling all the folks in Tin Can Valley about Jesus."

The Christmas dinner was greatly enjoyed by mother and son, and there was enough food given them by the mission to last for a long time. After the meal, Jimmie was very quiet. Suddenly he rose, puzzled.

"Mother, do you suppose those people up in the nice and pretty homes know of Jesus?"

"Of course, James."

"But how can they? They never told us. Maybe they don't know. I'll tell them." And before his mother could

stop him, he had pulled on his cap and rushed out into the blizzard.

Fighting bravely against the fierce wind and stinging snow, the lad made his way up the hill and across the streets to the big white houses on the hill crest. A lady gazed curiously at the ragged waif who had rung her doorbell.

"Missus," he ventured, removing his cap, "do you know Jesus?"

Too astonished to answer, the woman only stared at the boy.

"What is it, wife?" A man appeared behind the woman.

"Did you ever hear about Jesus?" the lad repeated.

"Of course, sonny. Better come in and get warm before you freeze to death," the man said as he pushed the door open.

Jimmie looked inside. He could see the glowing fireplace and feel the inviting warmth, but he shook his head. "No, sir. If you know, then I must tell others."

On and on he sped from house to house, always asking the same question and invariably receiving a yes reply. At last he came to a house much larger than the others and much more beautiful. A man with an annoyed countenance opened the door and Jimmie asked his question.

"Have you ever heard of Jesus?"

"Yes" was the short reply. And the man was about to close the door in Jimmie's face when the persistent child leaned forward and asked the question that had been troubling his heart ever since he had been on the hill.

"Then why didn't you tell us down in Tin Can Valley?"

"Why— er— er," the man stammered. Then, noting the shivering form before him, his countenance softened.

Throwing his arm around Jimmie he said, "Come in, son, and we'll talk it over while you get warm."

"Oh, no, sir! I have to tell others. Jesus told all who know about Him to tell others. I must obey Him. Thank you, mister." And he tore himself free and darted out into the snow.

Recovering from his astonishment, the man ran down the steps. But the deepening twilight and blinding snow hid the boy from his sight. He was unable to determine which way the lad had taken. "He can't go far," he muttered. "He is almost frozen to death now." Plunging into the blizzard, he pressed forward. Finding no trace of him, he at length ventured to a door and rang the bell. "Has a little boy been here recently?"

"About half an hour ago," the lady who answered the door explained. "And I have been worried over him ever since he left. He will surely freeze."

Murmuring a hasty "Thank you," the man retraced his steps and rushed on. Finally, he saw a small figure ahead, crumpled in the snow. He ran forward. It was the little missionary.

"My boy," he said, grasping the child's shoulders and pulling him up.

"Don't stop me, mister," he answered, "I must go— on— tell— others." He swayed, and would have fallen, but strong arms were about him. The cold was too much for the thinly clad form. Rushing him into the nearest house, the man summoned a doctor while others rendered first aid. But it was too late. Jimmie's work was done.

The result? The wealthy homeowners were stirred. Hearts previously cold and indifferent were melted. Jimmie

had given his life so that they might know Jesus—and to know Him is loving Him and others.

The inhabitants of Tin Can Valley were provided with more habitable dwellings, the men were given work and helped to get a good foothold in life. The Hollow was cleaned up and made beautiful, and at the very top of the slope, a church was built whose steeple reached toward heaven. Over the pulpit were written these words: "If you know Jesus, why don't you tell others?" They were placed there by the man who built the church and encouraged and directed the work done in the Hollow—the man who found Jimmie.

Or should I say, the man whom Jimmie found.

If you know Jesus, why don't you tell others?

A Stolen Christmas

Charles M. Sheldon

In 1997, a multicolored Christmas in My Heart 6 came out—another lovely Currier & Ives old-timey illustration on the cover. One of the joys of compiling this series is getting acquainted with so many editors, publishers, and authors. For instance: the venerable editors at Christian Herald *magazine— one of the editorial treasures of our nation—have graciously opened their archives to us. One of their most revered editors was Charles M. Sheldon, author of one of America's all-time best sellers,* In His Steps. *He also wrote stories, such as the one in this collection, "A Stolen Christmas." What a provocative plot: To have your Christmas tree and all your presents stolen out of your front room!*

* * * * *

Careful now, John," said Mrs. Mary Gray, as her big, tall husband stood on tiptoe and leaned over to fasten a small object on the very top of the Christmas tree.

The object was a gilt paper angel, blowing a silver trumpet on which were the words, "Glory to God in the highest!"

John fastened it securely, after several trials. After descending the ladder and stepping back, he gave a deep sigh, and said, "How do you like it, Mary?"

"Lovely! Beautiful! Splendid!" said Mary, using up three of her best adjectives at once.

"Well, I hope it will do," replied John soberly.

"Of course, it will do. What makes you talk so!" said Mary with a tone of reproach.

"Well, you know it is so different from what it used to be. There are no happy surprises for the children any more. Rob has been teasing for that gun for two months, and he knows he is going to get it. And Dorothy picked out that speaking doll two weeks ago, and she knows what it is. And Paul opened the package containing his automobile when it came up the other day. There's not much fun getting Christmas presents anymore. It's an old story by the time you have them."

"You old growler," said Mary. "You are tired. Let's go into the library and rest. The tree itself will be a surprise, won't it? The children don't know about *that*."

"I hope not," replied John as they went out and shut the door.

They passed through the sitting room into the library and sat down on opposite sides of a reading table. Mrs. Gray looked a little anxiously at her husband.

"You don't begrudge the work of giving the children a happy time at Christmas, do you, John?"

"Of course not. You wouldn't think so if you saw me getting that tree. I wanted one thing that I got myself, instead of buying it, and you know what a job I had getting it from Fisher's Cove. I believe the children will be surprised when they see it. But it doesn't seem quite natural to light it up in the morning."

"We must, though. We promised them their presents in

the morning. You're sure you didn't forget anything?"

"Pretty sure," replied John gravely. "Want me to go over the list? High-class repeating rifle for Rob. Automatic speaking, singing, and walking doll for Dorothy. Real gasoline toy engine automobile for Paul. Two pounds of assorted candy for each. Then there is the warship, exact copy of the *Kansas*, with real guns and powder, for Rob and Paul together. Football and headgear for Rob. Reflectoscope for Paul. Card case for Dorothy, and two bottles of perfume. *The Bandit of the Sierras* for Paul. Complete china tea set for Dorothy, with electric lamps for the table. Besides what you hung up for me and what I hung up for you."

"John," said Mary coaxingly, "what was that queer-looking bundle you hung on the big limb near the window? Was that for me?"

"You're as bad as the children," said John, laughing. "What do you want to know for?"

"I can't wait till morning, John; *tell* me."

"No, ma'am. I won't do it. Can't you wait a few hours? It's almost eleven o'clock now. The children will be awake in six hours, and we will all come down together. That's the plan, isn't it?"

"Yes. Oh, well, I can wait. It's something pretty, I hope."

"I hope it is," said John anxiously.

"Because, John, you remember last Christmas you got me that patented dishwasher that broke everything into bits when you turned the handle."

"That was because I read the directions wrong and turned the thing backward," said John hastily.

"Well, I hope you have got me something lovely this time. I have yours."

"What is it, Mary? *Tell* me."

"You're as bad as I am. No, sir. You'll have to wait. There's one thing I feel sorry about, though; I wish you hadn't got that gun for Rob. I'm in mortal terror he will shoot himself or somebody else."

"Of course not. If he is going to be an American citizen he has got to learn how to handle firearms. He may be a brigadier general or an admiral someday."

"I hope not, John. Besides, I have been wondering a little lately if guns and warships are appropriate Christmas presents."

"Oh, pshaw, Mary! Anything is appropriate if you have the money to get it. The main thing about Christmastime is getting something. The bother is to know what to get. The gun won't hurt Rob any more than the candy."

"You got too much of that. Just think, John, two pounds apiece. And Uncle Terry always sends in such a lot of candy every Christmas."

"Oh, well, we can give some of it to Lizzie. She never has enough. Or else send it out to the poor farm."

"Yes, that's what we will do," declared Mary.

"Well," said John, as he rose, yawning, "let's have one more look at the tree before we go up."

He and his wife went to the door and opened it. John turned on the electric lights, and he and Mary stepped into the room.

At first, they could not grasp the obvious fact. John rubbed his eyes and opened them again. Mary ran forward with a sudden cry, and then stood in the middle of the room.

The Christmas tree was *gone*, along with everything

that had been hung on it and placed at its foot! Not a thing was left except a few broken strings of popcorn, two or three wax candles, a shred or two of gaudy tinsel, and bits of evergreen. The tree itself was simply gone.

Mary ran forward to the big window that opened on the side veranda. It stood wide open, and other fragments of the tree and its trimmings were littered on the broad window sill. In the middle of the sill, resting calmly on its side, was the gilt paper angel and its trumpet, the only thing left behind intact.

"John, oh, John, someone has stolen our tree!" cried Mary as the full enormity of the event became clear. She ran to the open window, but John was there before her. He leaped out upon the veranda. Bits of evergreen and small strings of popcorn showed which way the thief, or thieves, had gone, straight across the lawn, out to the middle of the road, and there the trail ceased.

"They had a wagon!" gasped John.

Mary had followed to the edge of the curb. "Quick, John! Run in and telephone the police station. They may catch them yet. Oh, to think of our Christmas—"

John was already in the house, snatching up the receiver.

Did you ever have to telephone to a fire station that your house was afire and you wanted the department to hurry up before the house was burned to the ground? Then you can sympathize with John Gray on this Christmas Eve as he waited what seemed to him like a whole hour before he heard a lazy voice say, "Yes, this is the police station."

"Say! Send a man or two out here quick. Someone has stolen our Christmas."

"What!"

"Send someone right out here quick. Our Christmas has been robbed, stolen, do you hear?"

"Yes. Stolen! What has been stolen?"

"Christmas!"

"Christmas *what*!"

"Oh, John!" broke in Mary, wringing her hands and crying hysterically. "Tell the man it is our tree—our tree! Our Christmas tree is gone."

"Tree!" roared John. "Christmas tree. Someone has stolen our Christmas tree. Do you get that?"

"Free?" came over the wire.

"No. Tree! Tree! Christmas tree! Send someone right out here, will you?"

"Out where?"

"Out *here*!"

"Where is it?"

"Oh, give him the name and number, John!" Mary cried again.

"John Gray, 719 Plymouth Avenue. Come quick, won't you?"

"All right. Be out there with the patrol."

John hung up the receiver and turned to Mary. She had sunk into a chair and was sobbing. At the sight, John began to recover some of his wits.

"Don't cry, Mary. The police will get them. They can't have had much of a start."

"But who would steal a Christmas tree? It might be some prank of the Raymond boys."

"No, I don't believe they would do that. Besides, you know Raymond never lets them stay out after nine o'clock, and here it is nearly midnight."

"What shall we *do*? How can we keep Christmas? To think of all those presents—" Mary broke down again at the thought.

"I hope the six-shooter and the warship will go off at the same time and kill 'em," muttered John darkly.

"And there was your present to me," said Mary with a groan. "Now I shall never get it."

"Maybe you will. I can get another."

"Oh, why couldn't you go downtown and buy some more things?" cried Mary suddenly.

"Too late," John replied gloomily. "Besides, the stores are all closing up. And besides, I haven't the money to buy any more six-shooters and real toy automobiles."

"But what will the children do?" asked Mary desperately. "Here we are without a single thing for them. It will break their hearts to have a Christmas and no presents."

"Maybe we could borrow a few of the Morgans'. They always have stacks more than they need."

Mary was about to reply indignantly to this levity on John's part when the patrol car arrived. Two officers came in, and John and Mary answered questions and showed

them the place where the tree had stood, and where they were sitting when it was stolen, and where all traces of it had ceased in the road.

After the officers had examined all the evidence and had departed, after solemn promises to do all in their power to catch the thieves, John and Mary heard the clock strike the half hour.

"We shall never see that tree again," declared Mary in resignation. "Now what shall we do? We must have *something* for the children. I am going to make some candy."

"It's past midnight," objected John.

"I don't care. I can make some from mother's recipe, in the chafing dish."

Mary went out into the kitchen, and John, after standing irresolute for a minute, went upstairs. He peeped into the boys' bedroom as he turned on the hall light. They were sleeping peacefully, and on Rob's placid face there was anything but the warlike look of a brigadier general or an admiral.

Mr. Gray turned out the light and went on up another flight of stairs to his den. He sat down at an old desk, pulled out various drawers, and took out half a dozen articles, wrapping each one carefully, and marking them with the children's names. He gathered them up and came downstairs.

Mary was busy over the chafing dish.

"I've thought of a plan," said John, spreading out the articles on the table. "You put the candy in their stockings, and one of these in each. Then we'll hide the rest somewhere and ask them to find them after dinner. There's that Chinese god Colfax sent me last year from Tientsin, and the little box of Japanese water flowers that has never been opened, and the fairytales Graves sent us from Tokyo. I've been keeping them for rainy days, and the children have never seen them."

"Just the thing!" exclaimed Mary with enthusiasm. "Oh, John, you are the brightest man—except when at the telephone. I never knew you to get a message straight yet. But what shall we tell the children about the tree?"

"Tell them the truth," said John wisely. "The excitement will keep them from thinking about their loss."

That was the strangest Christmas the Gray family had ever spent. Before five o'clock, three children were sitting up, wide awake.

Rob whispered to his brother. "I know what they've got. A tree. Father tried to sneak it into the barn two nights ago, but I saw him. Let's go down and turn on the light before Father and Mother wake up. I want to see my gun."

"And I want to start my automobile," said Paul, hastily climbing out of bed.

"And I want to wind up my doll and hear it cry," said Dorothy.

The three white figures stole downstairs with no more noise than that made by Rob as he fell over a rug in the hall.

They opened the door in the parlor and turned on the light and stared. Instead of a beautiful tree, they saw the well-known furniture of the room and nothing else, except three stockings hanging from the parlor mantel.

Their astonished exclamations awakened their parents. When they came down, the matter was explained. The boys looked very sober. But as the family sat down to

breakfast, Dorothy relieved the seriousness by leaving her place, going over to her father, and saying, "What if those wicked men had shot you and Mother. That would have been even worse, wouldn't it?"

"I believe it would, for *us*," said John Gray with a laugh that changed into a half-sob when Dorothy put her arms around his neck and kissed him.

They were all at breakfast when their nearest neighbor, Mark Raymond, came in. "Just read about your loss in the paper! It's the meanest thing I ever heard of. But I've found one of the things. I was out early and saw this bundle lying close in by the curb in front of my house, and it has your name written on it, Mrs. Gray."

"Oh, my present!" exclaimed Mary. It was the queer-shaped package she had asked John about. She hastily cut the string and unwrapped the package. "What is it?" she said when it was uncovered.

"It's a combination towel rack and shaving mirror and—"

But that was about as far as John got. Everybody roared, Mark Raymond with the rest. Rob got hold of the combination and tried to work it, and something caught his fingers and pinched them. They all roared again—except Rob. Mary laughed until she cried. When they could not laugh anymore, Mark Raymond rose to go.

"Well, no use to wish you folks a Merry Christmas. You seem to be having one all right."

"We've got one another," said Mary, looking mischievously at John. "I don't believe any other man in town would buy his wife a towel rack and shaving mirror combined."

John looked a little disturbed at first, then his face cleared up. "You see, Raymond, my wife is different from all the rest. She can take a joke even when it isn't meant."

Raymond looked at Gray with hesitation. Then he spoke suddenly. "Say, Gray, can you—would you and Mrs. Gray go to church this morning, if you had an invitation?"

"Church?"

"Yes. You see, I belong to the Brotherhood at church. You know Reverend Strong. Well, he is holding a Christmas morning service. Lots of good music and a short sermon. Mr. Vinge plays the organ. The English have Christmas Day services in their churches and everybody goes."

John Gray looked undecided. "Oh, I don't know. I'm not much of a churchgoer, as you know, Raymond."

"That's the reason I'm asking you," said Raymond with a smile. "Be delighted to have you come. Both of you."

"Why not?" said Mrs. Gray. "Lizzie will get dinner. No one has stolen our turkey. I saw it go into the oven. And I like to hear Strong."

Rob spoke eagerly. "Did you say Mr. Vinge is going to play the organ?"

"Yes," said Raymond.

"I want to hear him," said Rob, who was music-loving in spite of his warlike proclivities. "Can't I go?"

"Me, too," chimed in Paul.

"I won't stay here alone. I want to go too," said Dorothy.

"We'll all go," said Mary decidedly.

"I don't care," laughed John. "It's a queer Christmas to start with and might as well be queer to go on with. I never went to church on Christmas in my life."

"Won't hurt you," said Raymond, much pleased. "Sit with my folks. We are all going."

So an hour later John Gray and his wife and their children were in church with their neighbors, the Raymonds. John felt a little bewildered. But he had been more or less bewildered ever since he opened the parlor door to find the Christmas tree stolen. As the service went on, the beauty of it crept in upon him. The church was trimmed with wreaths, and up near the pulpit was a tree, shapely and benignant, with no presents on it, but lighted with small electric lamps, and tinged with white. Vinge, the blind organist, sat at his beloved instrument. What melody flowed out of it! The Christmas glory flooded his keys.

John glanced at his wife. Her face was wrapped with tender feeling. "Glory to God in the Highest," sang the children's choir. The fresh young voices were fragrant of Bethlehem and the Nativity. Gray looked along at his children. Rob, the warlike, was lost to all the world, his boyish face upturned to catch all sound, his eyes fixed on Vinge, his soul caught in the meshes of that blind man's harmony. Something choked John Gray. What if sometime his boy should be a great organ player! What fine children God had given him!

His glance came back to his wife. What a lovely face she had. What a beautiful mother she had always been. How devoted to her husband. How proud of him, in spite of his awkward blunders and many faults. He quietly reached for her hand and thrilled at the clasp of her warm, firm fingers. She smiled at him, and then together they listened to Phillips Brooks' most beautiful hymn, "O little town of Bethlehem / How still we see thee lie." A little later in the service they joined their voices with the congregation, as they sang "Angels from the realms of glory / Wing your flight o'er all the earth."

Then the sermon touched them. Even the children could understand it, it was so simple, and so clear in telling what Christ meant to the earth.

When the service closed in a quiet moment of worship, the people rose silently and went out. At the door, Gray exchanged greetings with several friends, and as he walked along home, he said to his wife, "Say, Mary, I liked that. Wonder why the churches in America don't have Christmas Day services more generally."

"It meant more to me than I can tell, John. Somehow I feel younger and happier. Doesn't that seem queer, when all our presents were stolen, except mine?"

They both laughed.

"We have each other," said John gently.

"And the children," said Mary.

"And the children," John agreed.

After dinner, the children hunted for the other articles their father had hidden. They were simple things, saved for rainy-day use, but they were real surprises. Near the big window in search of her present, Dorothy discovered the gilt angel with the trumpet. It had lain peacefully there during all the excitement.

Mrs. Gray put it on the mantel over the clock. Later in the day, while the children were out in the kitchen cracking some nuts Rob had stored in the barn last fall, she said to John, "I believe that angel has something to do with our happiness. Doesn't it seem strange to you, John? It was a dreadful loss, but we don't seem to be feeling so dreadful about it. After all, the boys never got the gun or

the warship. And they don't seem to feel so very bad."

A shout of laughter came from the kitchen where some of the Raymond children were visiting with the Grays and showing them their presents. And they could hear Dorothy say in a tone of superiority, "But that's nothing. We had a *burglar* in our house last night!"

"It does seem strange," said John. "The police just phoned that they can get no clue to the robbery. It's been a very different sort of Christmas. Mary, what were you going to give me in exchange for the towel rack?"

"Go up to your den and find it," said Mary shyly.

John went up, two steps at a time. On his writing desk he found it—a photograph of his wife, framed in an old-gold oval frame that had belonged to her mother.

When he came down, he was met by Mary at the foot of the stairs.

"Oh, John, do you like it? And it's a surprise to me too. I thought it was gone with the rest. But when you went through the window, I saw my present to you on the veranda and saved it for a surprise. Do you know another woman in town who wouldn't have told?"

"No, I don't. And I don't know another like you in any way." And John kissed his wife, who actually blushed for happiness.

Later in the evening, as the family sat in front of the fire eating nuts and apples, Mrs. Gray asked Dorothy to go into the library and bring a box she would find on the big table. When it was brought in, Mrs. Gray asked Dorothy to open it. Faded tissue paper wrappings came off. And there lay an old-fashioned doll, dressed in India muslin, with quaint ribbons under a Converse hat. Dorothy was overcome.

Mary whispered to John, "Bessie's doll. I haven't had the heart to give it to anyone until today."

A tear fell on John's hand as the memory of their first child crept into the firelight and softened the glow of that new Christmas. Later, when the children were asleep, Dorothy, hugging the India muslin doll up to her cheek, John and Mary came down and sat by the fire.

"After all, we have had a beautiful day, Mary," John said. "We have one another."

"And the children," said Mary.

And the firelight flung a flame a little higher than the rest so that the trumpet of the gilt angel stood out very clear with the words, "Glory to God in the highest and on earth peace among men in whom he is well pleased."

Then there stole into the hearts of John Gray and Mary Gray, his wife, at the close of that blessed Christmas Day, something more like the Peace of God than they had ever known. The Christ Child meant more to them than He had ever meant. And in their hearts they both yearned for a better life, glorified by Him who is the peace of those whose hearts are restless, and the joy of those whose hearts are sad.

His Last Christmas

Joseph Leininger Wheeler

As is true with so many others, I mistakenly assumed my folks were so strong they'd remain healthy and vibrant for a long time yet to come. As for my father, I considered him borderline indestructible. But then came warning tremors, a debilitating disease that swept through a hospital facility. In no time at all, the unthinkable happened, and one after another of us trekked into Dad's room to get his patriarchal blessing. It is a sobering experience to look at your father's face on a pillow and realize that when death takes him, age-wise, you are next on the family tree! It was for this reason I wrote "His Last Christmas" for our green-covered seventh collection in 1998. My only regret is that I didn't share more of my appreciation with him before it was too late!

The following story was inspired by the last few weeks of my fathers life.

* * * * *

W ho is he?"

"*He?* Oh, you're new here, aren't you? He's been here for a month or so now. One of the good ones . . .

never complains; makes up for those who do their best to make our lives a living hell."

"But who is he—doesn't he come with a name attached?"

[Laughs.] "Of course he does! Sorry. He's Mr. Abbey."

"*Mister?*"

"Oh, I know it is a bit unusual, calling him 'Mister' when we refer to most everyone else by first names, but I can't really explain. In time—as you take care of him, talk with him, watch him—you'll know why we call him Mister."

"Now you really have me curious. . . . Is he kind of, you know, old-school formal?"

"Well, yes and no."

"Y-e-s?"

"Let's see, how can I put it? . . . I don't really know myself why it's so, because we have lots of other old men here, and we call 'em all by first name, old school or not. So it's not just his age—it's something more."

"Must be quite a bit more."

"Yes, you could say that. . . . I remember the morning he was admitted. He was wheeled in, and I helped to lift him onto the bed. He is very thin and doesn't weigh much. Has almost no power left with which to move himself. Oh, it's sad! . . . Yet he's not weak inside. Inside, he is probably the strongest person of us all."

"Now you *have* got me intrigued!"

"Is this a good time to talk?"

"Yes, I don't clock in until the afternoon shift. Take as much time as you can spare."

[Leans back in her chair, a faraway look in her eyes.] "Let's see, where was I—Oh, that first morning! . . . No

way I can ever forget it. He didn't say much (he doesn't say much). But his *eyes*! His eyes followed me as I moved around the bed and elsewhere in his room. His eyes were friendly—and there was just a smidgeon of a twinkle in them—but they also revealed a reserve I'm not used to in our patients here. They seemed to be weighing me, trying to size me up! That shocked me, because—"

"—most of the others think only of themselves and their problems?"

"You got it! And many of them are darn angry about being here, about being dropped off here by their families, about being defenseless—totally at our mercy—about knowing, deep down, that things will never get any better for them—*that they will die here.*

[A long pause, while she struggles to regain her composure.] "Yes, that's the worst of it. It's a lot like a dialysis wing I worked in a few years ago at Community General. We knew, and they knew, and they knew that we knew, that things were unlikely to get better—or not for long, that is. Almost all of them we'd see died. It broke my heart, so many of them were so young! I finally—finally had to leave. For some dumb reason, I thought it would be different here."

"Well, isn't it?"

"Yes, it is different, but not much. In dialysis, the body is shutting down on them. Occasionally, we'd see a miracle—a new drug, a new procedure, a new diet, healing from within by a higher power than medicine. . . ."

"You believe in God?"

"Yes, I do; no small thanks to Mr. Abbey . . . but that's another story. In dialysis, miracles sometimes happen, and I guess all of us, deep down, hoped a miracle would occur with each of those patients we came to love the most. But it's worse here: with age, there can be no miracle short of the Second Coming. Once the body begins to dismantle its white blood cell armies, once the inner organs begin to wear out, once the strength begins to ebb away—it's only a matter of time."

"You make it sound depressing. . . . I'm—I'm beginning to wonder if I should have come here."

"Oh, no! I guess I haven't done a very good job of explaining myself. There is a difference here—or, rather I should say, there *can* be a difference. There can be a beauty, strange as it may seem, in one's last moments. When one's inner spirit really shows through."

"I think you've lost me."

"All right, see if this helps. Several weeks ago, Charlie, a bone cancer case, was screaming night and day. You literally could not get away from his voice. He was in pain, great pain (every breath hurt), and he made sure every one of his breaths hurt us too—all of us! Charlie was angry at life, angry at us, and angry at God. And none of this anger did he keep inside of him—that was not his nature. He was terribly self-centered. His room was next door to 202—Mr. Abbey's room."

"Oh, the poor man!"

"I haven't told you the half of it! Two doors down the hall, on the other side of Mr. Abbey, was another screamer—a woman. She wasn't dying, but, oh, how we wished she would! A fouler-mouthed patient we have never had here. Hour after hour, she would rant and rave, screaming, raging, laughing maniacally. And every other word was a four-letter one."

"And in the middle of this was your Mr. Abbey. How did he take it?"

"Let me tell you. One night I subbed for a friend and took her graveyard shift. Normally, midnight to eight o'clock is the quietest of the three shifts, but not *that* night. Both of those patients were virtually out of control. In the midst of it, my nerves on edge and wondering if I could possibly stand one more day of it, I walked in to Mr. Abbey's room to check on him and turn him (he doesn't have enough strength left to even turn over)."

"Oh, how sad!"

"Sad, indeed! Well, he was wide awake (how could he *not* be? Nobody slept that night.). I walked to the head of his bed, and he smiled. I was about to ask him how in the world he could endure it, then I looked into his eyes, and they were filled with concern *for me!*"

"No!"

"Yes, it staggered me. In his quiet and kind voice he said, 'My heart goes out to you and all the others you work with. You are probably wondering, *Is it worth it? Could any amount of money possibly compensate for* this?'

"Well, I smiled a rather sickly smile and said (I had to speak rather loud in order to be heard), 'To tell the truth, Mr. Abbey, the thought *had* crossed my mind.'

"There was a long pause as we both listened to that discordant duet. Then he said, 'I feel sorry for them both.'

"Disbelievingly, I sputtered out, 'For *them?*'

" 'Yes,' he answered quietly, '*them.* Mr. Zingfeldt has no faith in God to help carry him through. He can't possibly, judging by what he says—'

" '*Screams*, you mean!' I retorted.

"He smiled. 'Yes, *screams* is correct . . . and the other—Mrs. Wilson, is it not?'

" 'Yes.'

" 'Mrs. Wilson must not believe in God either, or she would not continually take His name in vain.' A look of pain came over his face. 'That is what hurts me deep down inside, every curse against the God I love and serve hurts. More than hurts. Not because I can't handle it, but because she is in such need of the Lord, of a friend. Were I able to move, I'd try to talk with her, offer to be that friend. Same with Mr. Zingfeldt . . .' Then his kind, loving eyes softened, and he said, 'But *you* could be that friend.'

"Almost horrified, I spat out, 'Me? You've got to be kidding! I'm not sure I still believe in God. And this nightmare we are both forced to endure isn't helping any, that's for sure.'

"There was a long silence, then he said, 'Miss Andrews, would you care to tell me more? This isn't'—and here his eyes twinkled impishly—'a very busy time for me. . . . I have time to listen if you'd care to tell me why you feel as you do.'

"Well, I can't really explain it, but knowing Mr. Abbey had been a minister, I figured *Why not? This night is such a hell; maybe he can bring back some sense to all this—perhaps even to my life itself.* So there by his bedside I told him the story of my life—it has not been a happy one. Several times I broke down and wept. Tears trickled down his face too. My handkerchief did double duty that night. Mr. Abbey was not at all judgmental about the mess I'd made of my life; he just looked at me with his kind and loving eyes.

"It took a long time to tell, and why I'm telling *you* all

this, I don't really know; but somehow I feel I can trust you with it."

"Without question. I *promise*. . . . So what happened next? Do you mind telling me the rest of the story?"

"Not at all; might as well finish what I've begun. I spoke to him on and off throughout that awful, yet strangely wonderful, night. Each time I'd complete the rest of my rounds I'd return and we'd talk some more. If ever a person walked side by side with his Lord, surely Mr. Abbey does. Before daylight ended that sleepless night, he brought me back to God—gave me a hope, a reason for living. . . . I've started going back to church."

"I'm—I'm a bit curious. . . . Did you become that friend?"

"Now you put *me* on the spot! Well, yes, I felt I could do no other. I *tried*."

"And failed?"

"Perhaps; yet perhaps not. Mr. Zingfeldt was Jewish and felt that if God would let one-third of his race be snuffed out during Hitler's holocaust, then either that God was not the God the Jewish people have worshiped for thousands of years or, worse, perhaps that perceived God didn't even exist. Believe me, our dialogue got beyond my depth often, and I'd have to get back to Mr. Abbey to seek counsel. It was a strange triad. Then Mr. Zingfeldt entered into his final agony. We gave him powerful drugs because of the excruciating pain. His skin turned blackish and, about a week ago, he died."

"Do you feel you got through?"

"I don't really know for sure. I like to think so. Don't have much to go on, though, for he was so drugged during those last days he lost all sense of reality. But I was with him at the end. Just before he breathed his last rasping, gasping breath, awareness came back into his eyes, and he tried to say something—I never knew what. I reached for his hand, and I felt an answering squeeze (it must have taken his last tiny reserves of strength); he tried to smile . . . and then he was gone."

"And—and the woman?"

"Mrs. Wilson? I had less success with her. She'd just scream at me, curse me—she seemed demon-possessed. Just last Thursday we had her transferred. It was either her or us. So I guess I failed with her."

"Perhaps. Only time will tell."

* * * * *

"Hi there, Janet. It's beginning to look like Christmas."

"It *does,* doesn't it! I was head of the decorating committee this year. First time for me; before, I never felt like it, not knowing for sure if I even believed in Christmas—or Christ. But now I feel differently. I'm filled with so much joy I can hardly contain it."

"I can tell by your laugh. Every time I hear you my day seems brighter—your laugh is so infectious."

[Laughs.] "You're kind; others describe it in less flattering terms. . . . But the place does look festive at that."

"And the Christmas carols—is that your idea too?"

"Yes, it seemed like the proverbial horse and carriage—didn't seem right to have one without the other. Oh, by the way, have you been down to Mr. Abbey's room lately?"

"You mean, have I seen the decorated wall everyone's been talking about?"

"That's it! Isn't it something? I understand some of the family put it up. Wasn't easy, as they had to wear masks. So sad about Mr. Abbey's staph infection. He has more company than anyone else in the whole place, and it has made it so much harder for them to talk with him and tell him how much his life has meant to them. . . ."

"That's hard—'has meant.' It won't be long now, will it?"

"No, sorry to say. . . . By the way, Janet, you haven't asked, but I felt if Mr. Abbey could turn your life around, well . . . maybe, just maybe, he might be able to salvage mine. I didn't see how anyone could possibly mess up more than I have—three divorces and two live-ins."

"Not that I really needed to ask. I can tell it by your face."

"You noticed?"

"Couldn't help it."

"Well, yes. Only I was a harder nut to crack than you: it took weeks before Mr. Abbey brought me . . . he brought me . . . to . . . to, uh . . ."

Susan reached for her hand. No words were necessary.

After a long pause, Janet changed the subject. "Back to that wall! As you know, the family put up on it most of the jobs and roles Mr. Abbey has had during his long life. I was so intrigued that I memorized them. Let's see if I can remember them all: salesman, tailor, lumberjack, farmer, teacher, minister, counselor, missionary, administrator (did you know he's even been a college president?), band director (evidently he is an accomplished musician himself, both as a vocalist and with various musical instruments), choir leader, painter, devoted husband and father—oh, the list could go on and on! Everybody has been down there to look at it!"

"Kinda sad, isn't it, Janet? Now that we know about his long and successful life, we respect him for it. But don't you suppose that every patient in this place comes to us with a similar story, if we only knew it? Oh, perhaps not as grand as Mr. Abbey's, but some might come close. In fact, I sometimes wonder . . ."

"Wonder what?"

"Oh, uh, well, I sometimes note how we treat most of our patients. We treat children nicer and with more respect than we do them! And I wonder whether or not we would act differently around them if we knew their life stories . . . the way we know Mr. Abbey's."

"Hmm. You may have a point there. . . . I'd never thought of it that way. To so many of us, they are not really people at all, but jobs, paychecks, rather unlovely (and often smelly) specimens of not-long-for-this-earth humanity. What a difference it would make if we went to the trouble to really know them!"

* * * * *

"Happy New Year, Susan!"

"Happy New Year to you, Janet."

"Sad, huh?"

"You mean about Mr. Abbey, of course. Very!"

"Did—did you get in to see him before Christmas?"

"Of course, but it wasn't easy, with so many others

wanting to do the same thing."

"True indeed. I wasn't surprised by the many visitors who came, but I *was* surprised by how many of our co-workers found it necessary to visit that room, surgical mask or not!"

"And did you—did you hear him, uh—"

"—hear him play his harmonica . . . for the last time?"

"No, but I had heard him play before. But I heard it was *so sad*—everyone knew it was the last time. Stephanie told me Bob had to help hold up his harmonica. I'll—I'll never hear a harmonica again without thinking of him."

"Did you look at him?"

"Did I *what?*"

"Did you ever *really* look at him?"

"Oh! I think I know what you are driving at. You mean, his face."

"Yes."

"I did indeed. It was . . . uh, in a way, beautiful. A rather strange word to use, isn't it, in connection with a man's face (especially an *old* man's). But it's true, nevertheless. Strangely enough, several weeks ago the realization hit me that we aren't responsible for our faces when we are young, but we *are* when we get old! Look—intently study—any given face in this entire complex, and you will see truth, reality. . . . Whatever is inside has now seeped through into the face. It can't be hidden, not even by plastic surgery, for no plastic surgeon yet has been able to restore the inner ugliness or evil that can be reflected through one's eyes."

"I hadn't thought of it, but you're right."

"Yes, no matter how handsome or beautiful you were when young, you will be ugly—even repulsive—when old, *unless* you have been beautiful inside."

"True enough! And, on the other hand, even the plainest while young can be beautiful when old."

"Like Mr. Abbey."

"Like Mr. Abbey—not that he was necessarily plain when he was young."

"When did you see him for the last time?"

"Well, not at the very last, for his family was there until the very end. His wife was there a lot—she came to see him as regular as clockwork."

"An old-fashioned romance, they say. . . . Been married more than *sixty years!*"

"Yeah, they don't make them to last like that anymore."

"More's the pity."

"No one knew when he would go; we only knew it would be soon. That last night his daughter, responding to a sixth sense that told her time was running out, made a flying trip to see her father. She took one look at him and knew that *this was it.*"

"We *all* knew. No matter which hall you were in, it was all the same: we didn't speak with mere words—it hurt too much—but if ever eyes mourned the truth, they did that last night.

"I had found an excuse to get down to his room Christmas Eve. The room was full of Christmas cards. The flowers people sent were shared up and down the hall, making it the most festive wing in the place! Several church groups came through the building, singing Christmas carols. (I heard later that each one lingered longest just outside his door.) During one of these I happened to be in his room when he first heard their voices. How his eyes brightened! In fact, the most apt word I can use to describe it is 'radiance.' On his face was a look of radiance not of this earth. He turned to me, and said simply, 'I've always loved Christmas.'

"Curious, I asked, 'Why?'

"He didn't hesitate an instant—he *knew*. 'Because it celebrates the birth of my Jesus on this troubled earth.' It was indeed *his* Jesus: none of us could possibly doubt that Christ was his all in all. . . . But how about *you*—when did you last see him?"

"Oh, it was about the nineteenth or twentieth, if I remember right. Anyway, as usual, I had to come back several times before I caught him alone. It's amazing how many of us sensed he was leaving and wanted a part of him while we still had him."

"Truer words were never spoken!"

"Well, when I came back in for the fourth time, there was in his eyes that look of loving, tender concern for me that always greeted me, only this time it was more intense than ever before, as if he sensed it was our last time together. He smiled, and said, 'This is my last Christmas.'

"I didn't know what to say, for I knew full well he knew that *we* knew it was indeed his last. He took me off the hook. 'I have no regrets, Janet.' (At my specific request he'd finally graduated from 'Ms.' to my first name). 'The Lord has given me a full life, and I am ready to go. And He has given me such a warm and loving family. Actually two of

them: my biological children . . . and my children of the spirit, such as you. You are what I find hardest to leave. But it is time. My body'—and here he looked down ruefully to his strengthless arms—'is closing shop on me. Not too long from now my faithful generator will flicker for the last time, and then go out.'

"I could not trust myself to speak.

" 'And the next face I see will be that of Jesus!' What joy was in his face and voice! 'And,' he continued, 'in that world without pain, aging, and death, I want to see all my loved ones again. Will you promise to meet me there?'

"Too overcome to even speak, I could only nod mutely. Then George came in, and our last shared moment was over."

Breaking the long silence that followed, Susan said, with trembling lips, "The night he— he— he— left us, I was on duty. We all knew it was coming, coworkers and patients alike. There was an incredible hush. I don't remember a sound except soft footsteps down the hall. I could almost hear the feathered sibilance of angels' wings.

"Then . . . Maria (remember how crusty and sarcastic she used to be?), well, Maria came around the corner, and one look at her face told me everything. *He had gone.*

"I took one look at her tear-stained cheeks and took her into my arms, and I wept. We *all* wept."

* * * * *

Today life goes on in those halls, but not life ever again as it had been before he came. He came with but one stub of a flickering candle, and left a glow warm enough to light the world.

Legacy

Joseph Leininger Wheeler

The calendar pages turned again, and it was 1999. Every-where, it seemed Y2K was in the air. Dire calamities were pre-dicted for when the date changed from 1999 to 2000. How could digital gadgetry function without rewiring everything be-fore the numbers turned?

Only twelve months after God gifted me with "His Last Christmas," He inspired me to write its companion piece, "Legacy," and those precious blocks are still with us—amazingly intact after almost two hundred years.

* * * * *

It was cold and foggy that bleak December day on the Oregon coast. But inside my aunt's farmhouse living room it was cheery, and a hot fire crackled in the big black iron stove. On the mantel was a stack of Christmas cards and letters, and in a corner a small Christmas tree.

Suddenly, around the corner stalked Mr. Tibbs, a proud old tomcat of venerable years and uncertain ancestry. But lack of pedigree had never bothered Mr. Tibbs; in fact, he reveled in his mongrel polyglot Americanism. He would establish the dynasty.

Called upon by my aunt to perform for me, Mr. Tibbs leisurely responded in his own good time, letting me know he condescended to do so, not because I was in any respect worthy of it, but because he owed my aunt one of his royal favors. Old as he was, he hesitated before wheezing his way to the stool top, licked his chops at the cheese my aunt held high above him, then stood up tall on his back legs to claim the prize, yet never for a moment losing his dignity.

After Mr. Tibbs had paid his dues, he descended from the stool and swaggered out.

In the quiet moments that followed, I wondered, *Do I dare bring it up . . . again? Surely, if she was receptive to my plea she would have responded long ere this. My uncle hadn't responded either—and now he lies in his grave up on that misty green hill overlooking the valley. Perhaps . . . I'd just better forget it for now.* So I said nothing and leaned back into the softness of the couch, dozy because of the alder-wood fire.

* * * * *

I was a boy again . . . and my heart was leaping within me because I knew we were nearing the ranch. The first gate loomed ahead, and Dad's Ford slowed and stopped so I could get out. This had always been my job. The long wooden bar slid back, and the heavy gate lifted and opened at last; then I stood there holding it while the Ford chugged past me and stopped.

Ever so slowly (for I was small), I struggled across the road, that balky gate fighting me all the way. After rein-serting the bar, I ran up to the car for the best part of all: riding on the running board to the other side of Frazzi's vineyard. Some days we'd drive up to the Frazzi house, and

Mrs. Frazzi, large of girth, dark of complexion, poor with her English, and robust with her belly laugh, would throw her plump arms around me, brag about how I had grown, and tow me over to the always overflowing cookie jar.

But not today. Down I leaped for the second gate, also of heavy wood. It too was a struggle, and resisted every inch, squawking all the way. Once again the Ford rolled past and stopped. Once again I got on the running board.

The next gate, of metal pipe and wire mesh, was easier. Overhead, I could hear the wind in the pines. Occasionally we'd see a deer bounding through the manzanita, madrone, and buckbrush bushes. Today the road was dusty, but sometimes there would be snow on it instead.

On the running board again, and jolting our way ever higher up the mountain, my heart beating so turbulently it threatened to leap out of me. At last, the big maple tree and the clearing. Thousands of apple trees to our left, and just ahead, at the top of the crest, was the walled home of the self-anointed "Old Man of the Mountain," Grandpa Rollo, and his jolly wife, Grandma Ruby, who was deaf.

All the way up that last hill, Dad laid on the horn. As he swerved around to the house, there they were, waving, Grandma saying over and over to Grandpa, "Wh-y-y-y, Papa!" and to each of us in turn, "You d-e-e-a-a-r soul!" Background sound was provided by barking dogs.

Up there on top of the mountain the seven-hundred-acre ranch stretched away, to my childish eyes, to forever. I would explore it later. First, though, we'd go through the gate, through the evergreen tree windbreak behind the rock wall, to the little rock house in the middle. The door always squeaked. Inside it was rather dark, but there on the

lip of the rock fireplace were the purring cats. As often as not, one of them would be leaning against the great wicker basket of blocks.

The wind might howl and the rain pelt, but inside that snug little cabin of a house, filled with so much love and laughter, with the fire in the fireplace and in the kerosene lamp's soft glow; with the fragrance of homemade bread, fresh applesauce, and cold milk just feet away; with one of the cats or kittens purring on my lap and the blocks already stacked into dream buildings—well, it was home; it was Shangri-la.

Then we'd hear other horns, other slammed car doors, each punctuated by "Why, Papa!" and "You dear soul!" Then more laughter as uncles and aunts and cousins poured into the walled enclosure.

Swirling mists blotted out the little cabin and the side house where we children stayed when we got older, with its swinging, banging doors with semi-clear plastic instead of windows, and, not far beyond, the outhouse with its abridged Sears catalogue and pesky wasps.

Years passed, and we flew in silver DC3s to places thousands of miles away. Places where bougainvillea bloomed in the patios, royal palms bowed in rainy-season winds and exhausting heat, and freshly cut stalks of bananas lay on the back porch.

But every once in a blessed while, the silver birds would bring us back home, home to the three gates, the "Why Papa's!", the "You dear souls!", the cats on the hearth, and the blocks.

Once, a new word entered my childish vocabulary. My grandfather had been hauled into court by a neighboring

rancher over water rights. The opposing attorney, attempting to diminish the value of Grandpa's ranch, asked the loaded question, "How much is your ranch worth?"

Grandpa's attorney, never missing a beat, stepped in and shot a question back. "Do you mean the value if it came on the real estate market, or do you mean its *esoteric* value?"

"Esoteric" was a big word for me, but after I looked it up in the dictionary and had Mom explain it, I thoroughly understood. The esoteric value was the greatest view in all the Napa Valley region, the multi-hued sunsets, the fog banks rolling in from the Pacific, the snow flocking the evergreens and apple trees, the little walled house on the mountaintop, the thoughts, the dreams . . . oh, how could one possibly put a value on all that? Ah yes, it was easy for me to grasp the attorney's question, for children value esoterically to begin with.

* * * * *

A door slammed, and I was jerked out of the past and into the present. I heard voices; my aunt was needed down at the barn. Then there was silence again, and once again I slipped backward into time.

* * * * *

A number of years had passed, and Grandpa and Grandma were growing old. The winters at the top of the mountain were hard and cold. The apple business was exhausting. Then came the news: the big ranch was sold, and they were moving down the mountain to a smaller place (eighty acres).

The next time we went to see them, we came to their one gate only a short distance off the paved road. There was a larger compound now, surrounded by a long mesh fence to keep the deer out. Initially, there was only a tiny cabin, but over time Grandpa built a big, beautiful brick home, a veritable palace compared to the older one! Out the broad picture windows one could look across the valley to a small lake. There were rocks and boulders everywhere, but Grandma Ruby determined, now that the children were grown and gone and the apple ranch had been sold, to transform her little piece of earth into a flowering paradise.

It would prove a never-ending task, and Grandma would have to wrestle like Jacob for every blossom, for every lacy fern, for every rosebud. Now, when we honked and drove in, scattering cats and kittens in our wake, chances are we'd have to get out of the car and search out the business end of the hose and tap her on the shoulder before we'd hear, "Why, you dear soul!" Then, looking over our shoulders, she'd exclaim, "Why, Papa!"

Then we'd haul our suitcases into the big new house. Inside, it was spotlessly clean—it was kept that way. And it was easy to do so, because to Grandma and Grandpa the new house was too grand to live in. They compromised by installing an iron stove in the garage and moving in there. The main house was reserved for the family—all nine surviving children and their throngs of grandchildren. Grandpa now did most of the cooking (the applesauce and nut bread) in the tiny little cabin, for Grandma had traded cooking for flowers. The beautiful kitchen in the main

house was generally used only when company came.

When we'd come into the big house, there in the large family room was the great fireplace, and there on the hearth would be the wicker basket of blocks. There were never any other toys—just the blocks. As a child I never really examined them or wondered how old they were—I just played with them. When my other cousins wandered in, they'd plunk themselves down on the floor and play with me.

As we got older, however, the siren call of horseshoes drew us outside where those authority figures, the men, were challenging each other, and trying to beat Grandpa. To us, a rite of passage was reached when we were deemed old enough to play. Every Thanksgiving, as the clan gathered from far and near, the clang of horseshoes could be heard all day long—except during dinner, when we all gathered around the long, groaning trestle table in the big house. Around that table we saw a side of our parents we saw nowhere else, for here they were still considered to be children by Grandpa and Grandma.

And how Grandpa loved to tell stories! Like the time cousin Billy sidled up to Grandpa in the orchard and drawled, "G-r-a-n-d-p-a . . . , I t-h-i-n-k I s-e-e a- a-a s-n-a-k-e." And, as Grandpa told it, he'd always counter, "Now, Billy, don't tell lies! You know there's no snake around today."

There'd be silence for a while, until Billy forgot about the admonition and once again sidled up to Grandpa saying, "G-r-a-n-d-p-a, I t-h-i-n-k I s-e-e a-a-a s-n-a-k-e." And again Grandpa would warn him not to tell lies, and again Billy would subside into silence.

Then Grandpa would grin as he remembered the third request: "G-r-a-n-d-p-a, I t-h-i-n-k I— *I SEE A SNAKE!*" And no matter how many times we heard the story, we always jumped a foot off our chairs when Grandpa got to the place where he galvanized a frightened little boy into action.

Then there were stories such as the one about a man who used to take a shortcut home, from time to time, through a graveyard. One dark and moonless night he was taking his shortcut, unaware that earlier that day a new grave had been dug for a funeral the following day. Well, here he came, *pad-pad-padding* along, when suddenly there was no path. *Whumpf!* He plunged into the open grave. After he got up and gathered his wits, he realized where he was and tried to climb out, but the hole was too deep. So he called out for help, loud and long, but no one could hear him. Finally, exhausted, he gave up and sat down to wait for morning.

(At this point in the story, tingles would be going up our spines as we waited for the next line.)

"Suddenly he heard someone coming: *pad, pad, pad— whumpf!* And another man fell in!" Pausing to make sure he still had his audience, Grandpa then proceeded to tell us that the newcomer paced round and round the grave, just as the first man had, trying to find a way out, but couldn't. In the pitch dark the pacing man hadn't seen the first man crouched in a corner. Finally, the first man got up and approached the newcomer from behind, tapped him on the shoulder, and said in a sepulchral voice, "You can't make it, buddy!"

Then Grandpa's voice leaped into the long-awaited punch-line:

"BUT HE DID!"

And we'd roar—even us kids, by now playing over by the fireplace with the blocks. And stories and jokes would continue to be told—and we never tired of hearing them.

When there was a break in the action, Grandma would give us haircuts. In those early days, there was no motor attached to the clippers. Rather, each time Grandma squeezed the handles together, a sheaf of hair fell to the floor. Those of us who were down the line a bit had to endure the heat generated by the clippers that got hotter with each haircut. Even worse, Grandma would occasionally yank hair out by its roots, and we would howl (or scream) to no avail, because Grandma couldn't hear our wails. Being deaf, she could only read lips.

After supper everyone would gather round the piano to sing. Grandma would gravitate over to the piano, put her hand on the soundboard, and seraphically smile as she felt the music! Later, games would be brought out, and Grandpa would challenge all comers to caroms—and he'd whop most of his sons. If they didn't let us kids play games with them, we'd play with the blocks.

Eventually, the clan would drive away, one car at a time, to the sounds of slammed car doors, shouted good-byes, shooing away cats, crunching gravel, and tears.

And so it went, season after season. Each time we came, I'd turn and gaze longingly up the hill before I opened the gate, toward the lost Shangri-la beyond the three gates. In all the years that followed, I could bear to return only once. But it was not the same. A multimillionaire from San Francisco lived there now and had built something at the top of the hill I cried to see.

* * * * *

Awareness came back to me gradually. The house was still silent, so my conscious mind picked up where it would rather not have. I remembered when it seemed best, because of the battering of the years, for Grandpa and Grandma to leave their Napa Valley garden spot and move north to Oregon, so that my only double relatives (my father's youngest brother, Warren, had married my mother's youngest sister, Jeannie) could be near enough to take care of them.

But now the rest of the family no longer came on holidays, and the Oregon coastal mist and rain kept Grandma inside a lot. I went to see them in Oregon only twice. It was not the same—not at all the same! They seemed a hundred years older than they had been before. I did not see the blocks—I was too old to want to play with them anyhow. Gone was the vitality, what the Spanish call *chispa*, that made being with them such an adventure. Finally Grandpa just let go. And not too long afterward, Grandma, bereft of her lifeline into the speaking world, followed him.

By now I had a wife and children of my own and was too busy to dwell much in the past. But there came a time some years later when I began to remember. When I belatedly realized that, of all the things our family had ever possessed, I longed for only one thing: those blocks! I wondered if, by now, they had been thrown away. Who, after all, in this hectic life we live, would care much about an ancient basket of battered-looking blocks?

It took years, years of wondering about those blocks along the long corridors of the night before I finally posed a question in a letter to my aunt and uncle. "Those old

blocks we used to play with—if they still exist—what do you say to giving a few to each grandchild who used to play with them?" I didn't really expect an answer . . . and I didn't get one.

But in recent days, weeks, and months, I had more and more often been carried back in my thoughts to that time so many years before when those blocks were the most important thing in the world to me, the most prized, the most *loved*. Funny how so many years go by before you realize what you value, what you'd race for first if the house were to catch on fire.

I heard my aunt come in . . . and my heart began shuddering. *Did I really want to know?* In the end, I knew that even if the blocks were gone forever, I just *had* to know!

Struggling to keep my voice from shaking, I asked the fateful question: "Aunt Jeannie, do you remember . . . uh . . . uh . . . those, uh, blocks we used to play with so many years ago? Uh, I was just curious . . . Whatever happened to them?"

Matter of factly, my aunt ended the uncertainty of the years: "The old blocks? They're fine. They're here."

"They're *here*? In *this house*?" I sputtered inanely.

"Yes. They're here."

Pausing to regain my equilibrium, I finally managed to say, "Uh . . . do you mind if— *Can I see them?*"

"Of course! Come with me."

In her bedroom, in the back of her closet, was a strangely familiar brown wicker basket—filled with old blocks. She picked it up, took it into the living room, then handed it to me.

I was so stupefied I could not talk. Lord Carnarvon himself, on first stepping into King Tutankhamen's tomb in Egypt's Valley of the Kings, could not have been more overcome than I—I, who had long since given up the blocks as lost forever!

I stared at them stupidly, unable to say anything that made sense. Finally, I sighed, *"I'd almost kill for these!"*

My aunt smiled for the first time.

Time passed, and I continued to fondle them, unable to stop touching them. Finally, I asked her if she'd ever thought about my request years before. She said that she had, and that the answer was no. Then, seeing my woebegone face, a smile as big as Texas spread across her dear face. "But you can have them, if you wish."

"If I *wish*?" I gasped.

"Yes, but there are conditions."

"What?" I demanded.

"That they always stay together, that they are never divided, that they remain in the family. *Always*. And that"—and here her smile grew even broader—"only when you find someone who loves them as much as you do . . . can you let them go."

* * * * *

When I returned home with those precious blocks, I carried them with me into the passenger cabin, not daring to risk checking them on the plane.

A few days ago, for the first time in my life, I really analyzed the basket of blocks I had for so long taken for granted. The basket itself is most likely well over a century old. In it, there is an ivory-colored shoe horn, a very old darning sock egg, and an accumulation of seventy-three blocks, representing at least six generations. Twenty-two uncolored alphabet blocks are so old that the corners have been worn round by generations of children playing with them. One, perhaps the oldest, has burn holes in each of four sides, and dates back to the early 1800s. One single "A" block, with color, dates to the 1850s. Twelve multicolored picture blocks (forming a design on each side) date back to the 1870s. Four very small blocks with raised figures date back to around 1890. Twenty-two alphabet blocks with raised colored lettering date back to about 1910. And one modern, nondescript, colored block dates back to the 1940s. How it got into the basket, I haven't the slightest idea.

Apparently, each family, for more than a century, added blocks to the basket. Undoubtedly, a number have been lost during the family's many peregrinations: from Massachusetts to New Hampshire to Western New York to California (not long after the Civil War), and many moves crisscrossing California.

In the end, I concluded I was glad I didn't really know for sure how old the blocks were. It was enough that my only surviving great aunt, her memory still razor-sharp in her mid-nineties, remembers playing with the blocks and thinking them "very old" even then. Are they per chance two hundred years old? I don't know. Were they played with by a distant cousin, Buffalo Bill Cody? I don't know. And the tree the oldest blocks came from? Was it standing during the Revolutionary War? Was it standing when the Pilgrims landed in 1620? I don't know . . . but it could have been.

In researching block history, I discovered that alphabet blocks date way back to the 1600s, when John Locke first advocated their use in his landmark educational book Some Thoughts Concerning Education, 1693. Thereafter, alphabet blocks were known as "Locke's Blocks." They crossed the Atlantic and were played with by American children during Colonial times. By the mid-1800s thousands of middle- and upper-class American families owned such block sets as those earliest blocks in our family basket. Friedrich Froebel, one of the German founders of kindergarten education, urged the adoption of alphabet blocks in that curriculum, which really hit full stride in America late in the nineteenth century (Andrew McClary's Toys With Nine Lives: A Social History of American Toys, North Haven, Connecticut: The Shoe String Press, 1997).

But more to the point, why do these simple little blocks mean so much to people like me? Perhaps the best answer is found in Dan Foley's wondrous book Toys Through the Ages (Philadelphia: Chilton Brooks, 1962): "The magic land of childhood, which was filled with delight, vanished with the approach of adolescence; so, too, did the toys. Only a small fragment of the millions of toys made in times past, even during the last century, remain to bestir our nostalgia and to record the heritage of childhood." Foley then quotes Odell Shepard, who wrote in The Joys of Forgetting (Boston: Houghton Mifflin, 1929): "Our toys were almost idols. There was a glamour upon them which we do not find in the more splendid possessions of our late years, as though a special light fell on them through some window of our hearts that is now locked up forever. We loved them with a devotion such as we shall never feel again for any of the things this various world contains, be they ever so splendid or costly."

* * * * *

A few weeks ago our Grey House high in the Colorado Rockies was about as Christmassy as a house can get: on a ledge was Dickens's Christmas Village; on the mantel,

twelve stockings; in a far corner, a tall evergreen, ablaze with ornaments and lights. Outside on the deck our multi-colored lights could be seen from ten miles away. But, for me, there was something that meant more than all these things together:

Yes, there was Taylor, our first grandchild, only seven months old, but intent on toppling the tree so that he could suck on each branch. Short of that, if he'd had his way, the lower three feet of branches would have been stripped bare. The only thing he showed comparable interest in were the blocks. He drooled on them, he sucked on them, and he took fiendish delight in swatting down the block towers we made for him. I can hear his joyful chortle yet! I would guess him to be one of the first children to have played with those blocks during the last third of a century. (Quite likely our son, Greg, was one of the last to have played with them during the late 1960s.)

So it was that as I watched Taylor play, I felt a soothing sense of the continuity of life, of the past joining hands with the present, of a long procession of ancestors magically shedding their wrinkles and beards, gray hair and hoop skirts, and all plopping themselves down on the floor with the blocks, as children once again.

As for Taylor, I wondered if he'd love them as much as I did, as *they* did. Probably not, for our generations (even I was a Depression baby) had very few things to play with, compared to the king's ransom in toys we shower upon children today. Which makes me wonder: *perhaps we were lucky, for we appreciated what little we had.*

So it is that never can I look at this basket of blocks without memories flooding in upon me—memories of Taylor, my son Greg, myself, my father, my grandfather, and a host of faded, tintype-photograph ancestors. Given that intergenerational bond, somehow it does not seem far-fetched at all to me to imagine Grandma's greeting her home-coming family in the New Earth by saying, "You *dear* soul!" to each of us, then turning to Grandpa with "Why, Papa!"—and Grandpa turning to me and saying, "Joe . . . did you, by any chance, bring the blocks?"

The Castle-Builder

A gentle boy, with soft and silken locks,
A dreamy boy, with brown and tender eyes,
A castle-builder, with his wooden blocks,
And towers that touch imaginary skies.

A fearless rider on his father's knees,
An eager listener unto stories told
At the Round Table of the nursery,
Of heroes and adventures manifold.

There will be other towers for thee to build;
There will be other steeds for thee to ride;
There will be other legends, and all filled
With greater marvels and more glorified.

Build on, and make thy castles high and fair,
Rising and reaching upward to the skies;
Listen to voices in the upper air,
Nor lose thy simple faith in mysteries.

—Henry Wadsworth Longfellow

An Ill Wind

Frederick William Roe

As I look back through the years of my life, I cannot help but remember the trauma caused by things I've lost or misplaced. Also, how awful I felt if somebody else's money or possessions were involved. I prayed—oh, how I prayed—that Christ would intervene and help me find what had been lost. He had often referred to lost things during His earthly ministry, so I felt comfortable asking for His help. Again and again, the Lord came through for me.

"An Ill Wind," by Frederick William Roe, is just such a story—and it involves not one, but two lost items.

When this story was written, $100 would represent about $1,500 in today's money.

Few people today remember Frederick William Roe's stories, but I feel privileged to have helped preserve "An Ill Wind" for posterity.

* * * * *

A telephone call for Mr. Wharton!" called the telephone clerk, turning from her instrument.

The *slap, slap, slap!* of a wide paste brush on paper that had been vying with the endless clicking of typewriters in the busy office ceased abruptly as the paper hanger left his table to answer the call. At the same instant the rasping of a buzzer beneath Tommy Reynolds's desk caused that young man to rise quickly and disappear through a door marked "private," into the manager's office.

"Who turned on that steam again?" demanded an irritated feminine voice in the main office. "It's hot enough in here to boil anyone alive. And the smell of that paste—ugh!"

"Of course the boss had to have it done the day before Christmas, when everyone is tired and mad and busy!" a girl at an adjoining desk exclaimed. "There weren't enough people and things to fall over without having a paper hanger round!"

"Perhaps," another girl suggested mildly, "the boss thinks it won't do for Crane & Company to have that big smoke spot on the wall any longer than is absolutely necessary."

Miss Babcock, the first speaker, was not to be soothed. "Well, *I'm* going to open a window and get some fresh air!"

Inside the manager's office Mr. Gregory was giving Tommy Reynolds his instructions. "Go right over to the bank with this check," he said as he wrote his name across the back of the paper.

Taking the check, Tommy hastened into the outer office. He paused at his desk, slipped one corner of the check under the rubber foot of a wire basket filled with orders, and began to put on his overcoat. At that moment Miss Babcock proceeded to gratify her desire for fresh air by flinging up a window nearby. A tremendous blast of cold winter air rushed into the room. Wild confusion reigned among the employees of the office near the open window. The air filled abruptly with fluttering papers and wildly grabbing hands.

"Put it down!"

"Shut the window, somebody!"

Tommy's flattop desk, nearest the window, suffered most of all. His order basket, piled high, contributed a fluttering deluge of sailing papers that, as Miss Babcock closed the offending window with an impatient bang, settled slowly to the floor.

The paperhanger, returning from the telephone, found himself just in time to prevent his freshly pasted strip of wallpaper, aided by the sudden breeze, from slipping to the floor. Since it was all ready to go on the wall, he deftly caught it and, slapping it against the plastered surface, quickly brushed and tapped it into place.

With his coat half on, Tommy Reynolds whirled about, his first thought of the check caught by one corner under the wire order basket. It was gone! Flinging off his coat, he joined the rest in picking up papers from the floor. When he had gathered all he could find, he placed the loose pile on top of his desk and searched them hurriedly. A quick glance at the wall clock showed that it was a quarter of three. If he were to get to the bank before it closed he had not a moment to lose.

He went through the pile of papers twice, but the missing check was not among them. Again he searched the floor; he examined the contents of the wastebasket and even dragged his heavy desk from its position to see whether the check could have blown under it. A second glance at the clock showed him that it was eleven minutes of three. The situation was becoming desperate. Tomorrow would be Christmas—and the next day, Sunday. Whatever Mr. Gregory's reason for wishing the check cashed immediately, it would soon be too late to get it cashed before Monday morning of the following week.

Tommy hastily appealed to his fellow employees, and they joined him in a search of other desks, piles of papers

and wastebaskets; but their efforts were fruitless. By this time it was so late that it was useless to think of reaching the bank before the doors closed.

Tommy told Miss Greene, the cashier, of his predicament. "I'll have to go in and tell Mr. Gregory about it before long," he said with a groan.

"It's too bad, Tommy," she replied. "Although it wasn't your fault altogether, yet it was careless of you to let a check get out of your hands even for an instant, especially after it had been endorsed and anyone could cash it. I happen to know all about that check. It came in the mail this afternoon from a man who has been owing us a bill for a long time. When the check came, Mr. Gregory was a little suspicious and called up the bank. They told him he had better get it cashed immediately before the account was overdrawn. So you see why he wanted to get it in this afternoon.

"Still," Miss Greene went on, "if it's cashed the first thing Monday morning, it can't make so very much difference. But—you *must* find it. If you don't, Mr. Gregory would have to stop payment on it at the bank and write Mr. Giltner for another, and the chances are that that gentleman would take advantage of our carelessness in losing it and refuse to send it again. And the firm would be out $98.61. Now go and tell Mr. Gregory just how it is—the sooner you have it over with the better."

Sick with apprehension, Tommy knocked at the manager's door. Fortunately, Mr. Gregory was alone.

"Mr. Gregory," Tommy said, plunging at once into his confession. "I slipped a corner of that check under my wire order basket for a minute while I put on my coat to go to the bank. Miss Babcock opened the window next to my desk, and the wind blew papers all over the floor. That check blew away with the rest, and I've looked everywhere for it. I can't find it."

"You haven't been to the bank yet, and you've lost that check!" cried the manager. "You don't mean to tell me—" The big man stopped abruptly and sat staring straight ahead of him. The sudden silence was ominous. Trembling from head to foot, Tommy stood waiting. The subdued confusion of the outside office was hardly noticeable above the ticking of the little desk clock as it measured the seconds into minutes.

"Go find that check, and don't come in here again till you do!" said Mr. Gregory suddenly.

Tommy turned, fled through the door, and collapsed into the chair at his desk.

There was much—very much—work to be finished before the holiday, and Tommy realized that until that was done he must postpone further search for the check. Sick through and through with apprehension and despair, he forced himself to bend to his tasks. An hour of hard work steadied him somewhat. By suppertime he had regained his equilibrium.

On this last day—the last night—of the holiday rush, Tommy knew he could expect little help or sympathy from any of the other dozen employees round him. For the past month the night work had been growing heavier. Beginning with eight o'clock, the hour for stopping had gradually grown later, until during the last week midnight had been reached—and passed—by some of the office force.

As Tommy returned from a hasty supper and the busy

evening wore on, it became apparent that the small hours of the morning would come before the last of the weary toilers should depart for home. Mr. Gregory was always among the last to leave; none worked harder than he. At midnight the light still shone steady and bright from his office.

Late that afternoon, in accordance with his usual custom, Mr. Gregory had given to Miss Greene for distribution among his employees a small pile of envelopes. In each envelope was a short personal note commending the recipient for faithful service during the past year and wishing him or her a Merry Christmas and a Happy New Year; there was also in each envelope a gift of money proportionate to the employee's position in the office. There was no envelope for Tommy this year, a fact that further increased his misery.

As the hour grew late and one after another of the office force finished work and left for home with a cheery "Merry Christmas!" Tommy's spirits sank lower and lower. Soon everyone would be gone, and his weary, hopeless search for that missing check must begin. Christmas indeed! It was already Christmas, he grimly reflected as he glanced at the clock. The hands were exactly together at five minutes past one o'clock.

A little later Tommy noticed with a slight start that the office was deserted. Except for Miss Greene and Mr. Gregory, everyone else had gone. Even as he glanced toward the cashier's office the light above her desk went out, the wire door snapped shut, and Miss Greene crossed the outer office to Tommy's desk.

"Tommy," she said, drawing up a chair, "I know just how you feel. You're discouraged, you feel like throwing up your job with the firm, and you think Mr. Gregory's a hard boss. But put yourself for a minute in his place. He's been working late every night for the past two months, harder than any of us. Then Clancy set a wastebasket afire, nearly made a panic in the office, and smoked the wall all up. And now *you* go and lose a bad-account check that he's been after for months.

"Now I'm going to tell you something that not another soul in the office, except Mr. Gregory, knows. I wasn't going to tell you for fear it would discourage you, but I think maybe it will help you instead. Robert, the young fellow who used to have your job, was a great joker and tease. One afternoon about half past two o'clock he was waiting outside the cash window while I finished counting out a pile of bills that he was to take to the bank. The last bill happened to be a new, crisp hundred-dollar note.

" 'Whew!' Robert exclaimed when he saw it. 'You're not going to faint at sight of so much money, are you, Miss Greene? Allow me to give you a little fresh air.'

"And before I knew what he was doing, he had grabbed an electric fan and switched on the current so that the sudden blast of air came across the shelf and almost directly into my face. That hundred-dollar bill went right up into the air. Robert said it sailed clear to the wall at the back end of my cage and then shot down toward the floor. I brought both hands down on top of the remaining bills and kept them from scattering.

"I was too thoroughly annoyed and exasperated to speak a word. It was dark near the floor at the back end of my cage, and I couldn't find the missing bill. Robert offered

to help me, but I was irritated and wouldn't let him. Instead, I sent him off to the bank with the rest of the money while I locked my cage door and searched every nook and cranny for that bill.

"At the end of a half hour I had to give it up. It was as if the floor had opened and swallowed it up. When Robert returned from the bank and learned that I couldn't find it he was scared, for he knew that it was his thoughtlessness that had done the mischief. The next morning he failed to appear for work, and we have never seen or heard of him since.

"Well, Mr. Gregory was very kind and exonerated me of all blame, but I felt that, next to Robert, I was responsible for losing that bill, and I made it up to the firm. It's two years now since that happened, and I had almost forgotten all about it. But your losing that check today brought it all back."

"That's the reason Mr. Gregory stopped calling me down all of a sudden after I'd told him about the check this afternoon!" Tommy exclaimed.

"Of course it was," replied Miss Greene. "He was thinking of Robert. Now, I don't want you to make the mistake that Robert made. Whether you find that check or not, you stick."

"Miss Greene, you've helped me a great deal, and I want you to know I appreciate it. It's when a fellow is down and nobody seems to care that it's hard."

"Yes, I know," said Miss Greene softly.

For a few moments after Miss Greene had gone, Tommy sat with his head sunk into his hands. He was very tired. He'd far rather go home and sleep than look for a lost check. The sudden roll and rattle of Mr. Gregory's desk top as it closed roused him. The door of the manager's office opened, and Mr. Gregory came out.

"Well, my boy, how are you coming on? Found that check yet?"

"No, sir, I haven't," Tommy replied. "I've only just finished my other work; but I'm going to find it if it's in this office."

"That's the talk. Go after it now, while there's nobody round to bother you. Report to me the first thing Monday morning how you've come out. Good night."

"Good night, sir," answered Tommy as the door closed behind his employer.

He was alone. Only the slow, measured tick of the big wall clock broke the silence. How different that ticking was from the nerve-racking sound of the busy day! Turning on all the lights, Tommy began his search. He rolled every desk aside from its place to bare the floor beneath, then put them back again. He searched thoroughly through every wastebasket. Finally, he entered Miss Greene's cage (she had thoughtfully left the wire door unlocked for him), and with a movable electric light began to peer between the tubes of the radiators, from end to end, and behind and underneath them.

As he rose from inspecting the last radiator he heaved a sigh of disappointment. There was only one other place in the whole office worth investigating, and that was under and behind the letter-file cabinet that stood against the wall just outside Miss Greene's wire cage.

Of course there were other possibilities: the check might have fluttered out the window, or fallen without

being noticed into one of the few desk drawers that were now locked. Or someone might have instantly recognized its value and, amid the temporary confusion, stolen it. But those possibilities seemed too remote to Tommy to be worth considering seriously, and he turned his attention to the filing cabinet.

The big case was heavy, but by moving each end out alternately a little at a time, he managed to hitch it as far as its own thickness from the wall. The dust of years lay thick on the floor and hung from the brown wallpaper behind it.

"Good chance to do a little cleaning up, anyhow!" Tommy muttered.

He got the office broom and dustpan and set to work to sweep up the dirt. Suddenly the wooden baseboard separated from the plastered wall behind with a startling *crack!* The sharp sound attracted Tommy's attention, and upon looking closer he saw that on either side of the filing cabinet the board had long been warped. With a thrill he wondered whether the lost check could have slipped down in the narrow space between the baseboard and the wall.

Steam heat from the radiators is what warped the board, he said to himself as he looked round for some thin, flat instrument with which to explore the narrow space.

The steel inks scratchers and the letter openers were all too short, the rulers were too thick. At last Tommy cut a long strip of stiff pasteboard that served the purpose admirably. Beginning near the corner of the room, where the crack started, he pushed the piece of pasteboard along the crack toward the filing cabinet.

Presently he struck some object, and, with his heart pounding fast, worked to bring it into view; but it proved to be only an old stamped envelope, and with an exclamation of disgust he cast it aside.

Continuing his search, he reached the wire partition that separated the cashier's office from the outer office. *Might as well make a good job of it while I'm at it,* he said to himself.

He got up from the floor and, going round to the inner office, continued his investigation of the crack. He had scarcely advanced three feet when his strip of pasteboard again encountered some obstruction. The next instant Tommy brought the object into view. For a moment he stared at it with widening eyes, then he pulled it from the crack.

In his hands he held, still crisp and stiff, *Miss Greene's long-lost hundred-dollar bill!*

As Tommy rose to his feet a little selfish choke of self-pity came into his throat. Miss Greene would have a happy Christmas now. Then, with a sudden impetuous rush, a fierce, startling temptation assailed him. No one could possibly ever know! He could make good the lost check, probably keep his position, and even get some pity from his fellow employees. From Miss Greene at least. Pity from Miss Greene? After *stealing* a hundred dollars from her? Why, she was the best friend he had! She had tried her best to hearten him when things had looked black and hopeless. And he was thinking of *stealing* a hundred-dollar bill that she probably needed a great deal more than he needed it!

Finding is keeping! he muttered. *But not when you know who the owner is. And anyhow, what kind of a fellow am I?*

The struggle was over. Tommy hurried to his desk and scribbled a note:

My dear Miss Greene, Merry Christmas! I found this bill at the back end of your office, in a crack behind the baseboard.

Tommy

He enclosed the note and the bill in an envelope, which, after he had sealed and addressed it, he placed securely in the inner pocket of his coat. Then he returned to his task of probing the remaining length of crack in the cashier's office. He quickly finished it, tried the board upon the other three sides of the other office, which yielded nothing, and finally brought up at Clancy's desk, where he slumped wearily into the chair. Dropping his chin into his hands, he stared moodily at the wide panel of fresh paper that the paperhanger had so recently put on the wall between the big windows.

"Mr. Gregory doesn't *mean* to be harsh. Why couldn't Clancy have waited till after Christmas to set his old wastebasket afire? That plain paper is too light-colored, but I suppose—"

His jumbled reflections ceased abruptly. His eyes suddenly narrowed and concentrated themselves on a dark-brown rectangular outline on the buff-colored wall in front of him. Silently, with a swift leap of uncertain hope, he drew out his pocketknife, strode over to the wall, and with three quick strokes slit down one side and across the top and the bottom of the dark, damp spot. Bending back the flap of paper that he had cut from the wall, he tried, with trembling thumbs, to separate its edge into two pieces. For a moment he thought that he held indeed only one thickness between his fingers, but presently it yielded, and he slowly peeled from the still damp inner surface of the wall paper—*the missing check*! It was somewhat blurred, but otherwise unharmed.

Pressing back the flap of paper against the wall, Tommy smoothed it firmly into place until the three slits were scarcely noticeable. Then placing the check beneath a blotter and a heavy weight, he sat down for a moment to let it dry out and to recover from his excitement. He glanced up at the clock. The hands showed half past two. As he was speculating on the extraordinary place in which he had discovered the lost check, the telephone rang with sudden, startling clearness in the silent office. To his astonishment, it was Mr. Gregory's heavy voice that came over the wire.

"Is that you, Tommy?" Mr. Gregory asked.

"Yes, sir," answered Tommy.

"How are you coming on? Found it yet?"

"Yes, sir, I have."

"Thought you would. Where was it?"

"Under a strip of wall paper that the paper hanger put on this— I mean, yesterday afternoon. It must have blown over and stuck face down on a fresh-pasted strip of paper, and he put it on the wall without seeing the check. I happened to notice the dark spot on the wall where the paste wet through the paper. But *Mr. Gregory*, I found something else! I found that hundred-dollar bill that Miss Greene lost two years ago. It was down in a crack between

the baseboard and the wall at the back end of her office. And I'm going to give her a Merry Christmas with it to-morrow."

Mr. Gregory's voice seemed suddenly to grow deeper over the wire as he replied, "Well, Tommy, if Miss Babcock hadn't opened the window and the wind hadn't blown in and, well, you know the old proverb, 'It's an ill wind that blows nobody good.' You get right home now, quick, and go to bed. And Tommy, listen. Before you leave, go into my office and raise the top to my desk—it's unlocked—and you'll find an envelope there for you. *Your envelope!* Goodbye, and Merry Christmas to you!"

Johnny Christmas

Author Unknown

Then came the year 2001 and our tenth-anniversary collection. Ten years! It was hard to believe that Christmas in My Heart® was still alive after ten long years had passed! I filled the anniversary anthology with powerful Christmas stories, none more deeply moving than "Johnny Christmas"—after all these years, even to this day, I've never been able to find out who wrote it or who first published it. All I know is that a copy came my way, I read it, and I was hooked. And it grows on me more each year that passes. Certain heroines grow dearer every year and every time you reread the story that they appear in. Hopefully, someday, someone will discover her origins.

* * * * *

Kate Holloway paused for a moment before a window filled with satin comforters. Pink and blue and yellow. Pale green and gray. The soft lights above brought out their shimmering beauty. A neatly scripted card invited, *Buy a Christmas gift for your home. Only three more shopping days.*

Kate was tall and slim and would have looked younger than her thirty years except for the harshness about her mouth. She stood in the thin sharp rain and thought savagely, *How can you buy a gift for your home when you have no home? Oh, walls, a roof, a low picket fence, a fireplace, sure.*

But just a house and a memory. She stared with bitter eyes at the comforters.

Was it a year ago—or a hundred years—since she and Tim had planned so gaily?

It had been a Christmas lovely to remember. Something for ten-year-old Johnny to have forever. Only he had not lived to hold that memory. Five days later, two days before Tim was to leave for overseas duty, Johnny had been killed. Maybe it wasn't Tim's fault that the car had skidded on the icy pavement, but Kate had wanted Johnny to stay with her. He had begged to go along, and Tim had said with some impatience, "We're only going to drive out to Janey's."

No use thinking about it now. No use remembering the cruel words she had said or the look on Tim's face, the helpless sound of his voice trying to explain. She had not seen him since, but she knew he was back and was living with his sister, Janey Lane, and her husband. Janey had not forgiven Kate for, as she said, breaking Tim's heart.

Janey had been her best friend when they were in school, and it had seemed natural and all right for Kate to fall in love with her brother. All that seemed long ago now.

Funny. She had planned to buy a comforter like the fluffy one there. The pink one. Johnny would have loved it on his bed.

Kate did not intend to, but somehow she found herself inside the shop. When she left, there was a bulky package under one arm, and her bank balance showed fifty dollars less. But bank balances were of minor importance now. Kate added to hers each month simply because she had to go on living, and work made it easier. As manager of

a small dress shop, she made a good salary and deposited most of it in the bank. There was nothing she could buy that would ease the ache within her.

She walked on. The rain had turned to sleet that stung her face and peppered the stiff brown paper under her arm. The wind swept against her in icy gusts. Up ahead her white house looked neat and clean—and uninviting. The windows were blank eyes staring at her. Yet she could not bring herself to leave the house, because there she felt so close to Johnny.

For the first time in weeks, Kate went into the room that had been Johnny's, and the pain was almost unbearable when she looked at the smooth bed. At the blue wallpaper with the band of white ships. The chest of drawers in one corner and the table where he had worked on model airplanes. The room was stripped of his personal things, but his presence was still there.

She put the package on the bed, the comforter spilling out with a gentle whisper. Kate touched it, and then said aloud, "What a fool thing to do, and why did I do it?" She left the room and closed the door behind her. Her lips were drawn into a straighter line, if possible. But she didn't cry. She'd stopped crying long ago.

She fixed her supper and ate with the evening paper propped up before her, pretending to read. On the front page was an article by the governor of the state, urging people to take an orphan for the holidays. "Let's have every orphanage empty this year," he said. "Let every child have a real Christmas."

Kate snorted. What an insane idea! Still, if Johnny were here—two little boys instead of one romping about the house . . . She closed her mind against the image of Tim.

She remembered a year ago. She had tucked Johnny into bed, kissed his hard little cheek, and said, "Tomorrow is Christmas, so you'd better hurry to sleep."

He smiled drowsily and murmured, "That's such a nice word, Mom. I wouldn't mind if my name was Johnny Christmas."

She had gone back to the living room where Tim waited, and they heaped the rest of the packages under the tree. Kate had written on the cards, "To Johnny Christmas," and laughed when she tied them on his gifts. And he had laughed the next morning when he opened them.

Kate washed her dishes, hearing above the noise of running water the sting of sleet needles against the house. The shivery sound closed her off from the rest of the world and magnified her loneliness.

She went to bed early, but not to sleep. She lay there thinking, and the item in the paper about taking an orphan child came back to her. She felt vaguely irritated. Surely children like that had a nice time at Christmas. She rolled over and pulled the blanket over her chin. Tomorrow, she decided, she would take the comforter back and send that money to an orphanage. She would send a hundred dollars.

But Kate slept late the next morning and was in a hurry, so she forgot all about it. At noon she sat at the counter where she ate every day. The girl who waited on her said, "You know, I think that's a swell idea the governor has."

Kate stirred her coffee and asked in dry irritation, "Wonder how many he is going to take?"

"Three, the paper says," declared a masculine voice behind her.

Kate's hand froze, and a cold trembling swept her at the sound.

She turned slowly, and there was Tim. He looked the same as always. Older, maybe, than his thirty-five years, and thinner too. His eyes, brown like Johnny's, were remote, and the impatience was gone from his face.

"Janey is going to take one," he added, and waited, but Kate ignored his words. Finally, he said in a kind of despair, "Kate, how long are you going to go on this way?"

The curve of Kate's lips could not be called a smile. "Why bother, Tim?" she said bitterly.

He answered soberly, "Because I happen to love you, Katie. Johnny's loss was my loss, too. It broke my heart. And people who love one another should help one another in the dark hours of trial. But I guess I have a life sentence to loneliness."

He paid for his coffee and walked out, and Kate sat watching his back. She knew it was true. Tim almost went wild at the loss of his child. He stood so lonely, trembling, and her blaming him added to the weight of his anguish and woe. What kind of woman was she, anyway? For a minute Kate caught a glimpse of her own ugliness and cruelty. But she swept it aside, being by now so comfortable living with her resentment and revenge.

It was snowing that evening when Kate went home. Huge flakes drifted lazily down and called "Merry Christmas" to her, though she steeled her heart against it. People all along the street were greeting one another, and the very weariness of their faces was happy. The evening paper carried pictures of children who were being adopted out for the holiday season. Kate hastily turned the page,

folded the paper, and dropped it on the floor.

She sat before the fire, her feet thrust out to the flames, eyes half closed, dreaming of seeing on the woolly rug a small boy with a hurt expression in his eyes. Johnny would not have liked what she'd been doing the past months. He would have said, "Hey, Mom, poor Dad. Why Mom, we're a family—no matter what happens. You and Dad . . . then me." He would have wondered at her harsh speech, her frowns, and the way she had turned the cold shoulder on her husband, who was bowed down with grief as much as she. More, for he had her to worry about, besides the anguish of losing a son.

She was relieved when the phone rang. The fingers of accusation were getting pretty close. It was Tim's voice, and though it was brisk and businesslike, it brought an ache to her heart.

"Katie, you've simply got to help me," he said. "Janey was called away to a sick friend, and there is this child coming any minute to spend Christmas. Rick went with Janey, so there's only me. I'll bring the child over, and we can talk there."

He hung up before she could protest, and Kate went back to sit before the fire and wait. She stirred up her anger. She tried to get furious at the thought of his bringing a child there. "How dare Tim think I could take a strange child, even for an hour!" she exclaimed.

She heard a car stop and steps on the walk. She hurried and opened the door before the bell could ring. The snow was falling thickly and it lay on Tim's shoulders and on the shabby coat of the child who stood beside him, a homely little girl with two straw-colored pigtails showing beneath

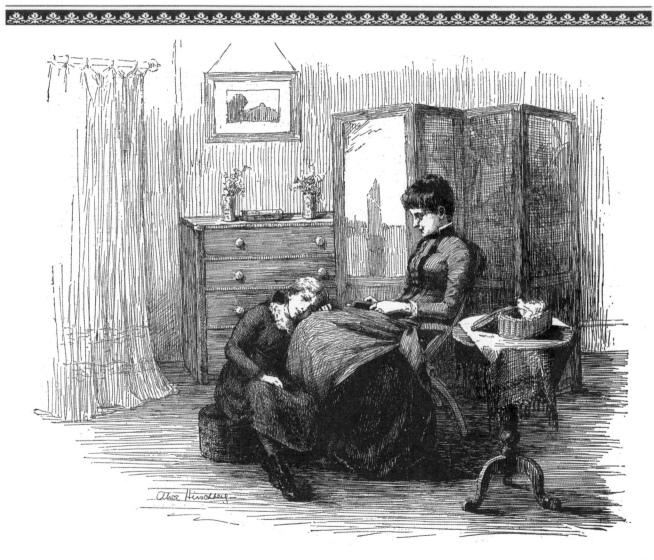

her cap. Tim put his arm about the child, looked directly at Kate, and dared her to deny them entrance.

"This is Johnny," he said.

Kate's fingers tightened on the doorknob. "Girls aren't named that," she said.

The little girl's eyes were wide and brightly brown. "I am," she announced. "Johnny Baker."

Tim brushed the snow from her coat and led her into the clean house. Kate closed the door and followed them. "Tim," she began, "you know—" But he seemed not to hear. She remembered how stubborn he could be. He was helping Johnny with her coat, and presently he was putting her into the brown bed that had held no one for a year.

Kate stood stony-faced, waiting until he came back. "When will Janey return?" she asked.

"I'm not sure," he said slowly.

Kate stared into the fire. She was trembling, and her hands were cold. "This was not kind of you," she said at last. "You could have kept her with you."

"At Christmas," Tim told her, "a child needs a woman. And you, I think, need a child."

"Maybe I do," she said bitterly, "but not just any child."

Tim reached out and caught her elbows tightly in his hands. "I've made you angry, Katie," he said. "At least, that's something."

He turned then, and a moment later she heard the front door close. She was alone in the house except for a strange child—a girl child—there in Johnny's bed. She went into the room and looked at the small figure humped beneath the covers. The satin comforter lay neatly folded on a chair.

The next morning the little girl stood just inside the kitchen door, watching while Kate made breakfast. "You don't like me, do you?" she said finally with the blunt honesty of a child.

Kate smoothed the tablecloth and deposited the pink sugar bowl in the exact center. "Why," she said, confused, "I hardly know you."

"But you don't like me. You don't like anyone." The words were a shock beating against the carefully built up wall. "Only maybe it's not your fault."

Kate was silent, pushing back the feelings of guilt and self-accusation that she knew were all too deserved.

They sat across the table from each other, and Johnny ate oatmeal and drank hot chocolate. Kate noticed there was a sprinkle of freckles across the snub nose, and her wrists were thin. Yet there was something oddly appealing about the little girl. She was like a little chipmunk, watchful, trusting, yet suspicious.

"How old are you?" asked Kate to end the uneasy throbbing silence.

"Ten," Johnny said politely.

Kate took a bite of toast. "Do . . . do you like the home where you stay?"

"No, ma'am." Johnny was quietly frank. "I hate it. Every one of the kids hate it."

Kate protested. "Why, I thought it was nice."

Johnny's eyes held pity for Kate's ignorance. She lifted her thin shoulders with a shrug. "Oh, it's all right, I guess, if you want to sleep in the same room with fifty other kids and not have a cat, nor nothin'. Only I want a room all my own so I can shut the door and no one can come in 'less I

say so!" She paused and looked thoughtfully at Kate. "Like yours. You got a place for all your things."

Kate changed the subject. "I have to work today. There will be lots of customers—next-to-the-last-day before Christmas, you know."

The brown eyes across the table glowed. "Oh, that's all right. I like to stay by myself. I'll straighten things up and cook supper for you."

Kate had thought she would call Tim and have him come and get the child, but somehow she could not dim the eagerness on that small freckled face. All day she worried. *What if the child set fire to the house? Suppose she set fire to herself? Oh, suppose any number of things.* She'd been a fool to leave her alone.

Kate hurried home that evening and paused with one hand on the gate. She had forgotten that the house could look like that. The windows were warm yellow eyes, inviting her to come in.

Kate's house slippers were by the fire and, in one corner, the radio was tuned to soft and murmuring Christmas carols. The small table in the kitchen was set for two, and there was a cheerful lived-in feeling permeating the entire house.

Kate went into her room, followed by Johnny. The silk comforter was spread on Kate's bed, and Johnny's fingers caressed it. Their thinness hurt Kate's heart.

"It's like a pink cloud, isn't it?" Johnny asked softly. "I didn't think you'd mind if I put it on your bed."

Kate took off her dress and reached for her old housecoat, but Johnny said shyly, "Wear the pretty green one."

Kate touched the quilted fabric. Tim's favorite. She had not worn it since last Christmas. Now she put it on slowly, buttoning it carefully, and tying the belt just so.

"It makes your eyes look green," Johnny said in wonder. Tim had said that, too.

They were sitting down to the table when the doorbell rang. Johnny went skipping down the hall to answer it and came back clinging to Tim's hand, her face lifted up to his.

"I've brought candles," Tim announced. "Do I get invited to eat?" His voice was uncertain. Kate tried to ignore the warmth in his eyes.

"If you like," she said, and Johnny hurried to put on another plate and light the candles.

"They look like Christmas," she said. Then she looked at Kate. "Will we have a tree?" She sounded confident, as though she was sure of being there. Kate felt Tim's eyes on her, waiting for her answer. Now was the time she ought to tell him to take this little . . . little waif . . . away with him. Tonight. Now. Surely he could find some other place for her. Kate thought she never wanted to see another Christmas tree.

She had the words all planned, but when she looked at Johnny's expectant face she couldn't say them. "Should we?" she asked.

"It's not Christmas without one," Johnny explained gravely. "I could go on out tonight and get one if you have to work or something."

"I don't have to go back," Kate faltered, her tongue playing tricks and saying things she did not intend to say.

"Then maybe we all can go," Johnny said happily. "Like a family."

Kate's fingers tightened on her cup. "I'm sure Mr.

105

Holloway—Tim—has to work."

"Nonsense!" Tim declared loudly. "Even a newspaper guy can get off on Christmas Eve. Especially when he has to buy a Christmas tree."

The next day was cold and clear with the heady excitement of Christmas riding the wind. The sun turned the crunchy snow into a carpet of diamonds. Johnny hopped along between Kate and Tim. "This is going to be a 'really' Christmas," she said happily, and shyly tucked her cold fingers inside Kate's gloved hand.

For an instant Kate held them tightly, remembering the feel of a little boy's hand in hers. Then, she said briskly, "Seems to me you need some gloves."

"I never had any." Johnny was matter-of-fact.

First of all, they bought the gloves—brown leather, fur-lined. Tim's big hands awkwardly smoothed them down on Johnny's hands. When he had finished, Johnny held them up for Kate's approval. "They are soft and warm and like a nice dream," she said softly, lights shining in her eyes.

The radiance in the child's face put a lump in Kate's throat, and she thought in quick indignation, *Why, every child has a right to things like that. They are necessities!*

Then they had to go and search for a tree that would be exactly right. "Not too tall, not too short, not too fat, not too thin," Tim solemnly explained to Johnny, and she giggled. Kate looked at her, startled to realize that she had not laughed until now. But Tim could always make a child laugh.

Suddenly Kate could bear it no longer. Planning just as though this were any other happy Christmas, as though nothing had changed. She went home and let Johnny and Tim finish their shopping alone, but the empty house made her restless.

The phone shrilled, and there was Janey's voice—a lot like Tim's—coming over the wire. Janey had not called for a long time. Now she said, "Kate, why don't you come to us for Christmas? You and Tim belong together. You must not continue to blame Tim. What happened was not his fault. It nearly killed him, too."

"I'm sorry, Janey, but you must let me be the judge of that. I suppose you'll want John—the child—this evening." Kate still could not bring herself to say the familiar name. Yet all at once she knew she did not want either the little girl or Tim to go.

"Child?" Janey said blankly. "What on earth are you talking about? I have two orphans here now, and I'm working my idiotic self to death. But we're having more fun than a barrel of monkeys. What child are you talking about, Kate?"

"Oh, never mind," Kate said, and she hung up not long after, puzzled and half angry at Tim for deceiving her. What an underhanded thing to do, foisting this child onto her and telling her that Janey was visiting a sick friend! She walked about the house, straightening things with jerky movements. So . . . Janey had been visiting a sick friend, and Tim had to help with a strange child! Kate tried to organize her twisted thoughts, for she wanted to be fair and to understand. But was this fair? Just what was Tim trying to accomplish? She thought she knew.

Kate poked the fire with vicious thrusts, and sparks flew out and disappeared in the chimney. She heard laughter drift up the walk, followed by the scrape of shoes on the

steps. They came in loaded with packages, and Tim struggled under the weight of the tree that would be too big. He had always done that. The fragrance of the pine tree spread in a fine cloud through the room.

Johnny hurried to the privacy of the back room to wrap her gifts. Kate stood looking at Tim, her lips tightly drawn, a strange feeling not quite of anger surging through her.

"So you know?"

"Yes, I know, Mr. Timothy-Fix-It," she heard her voice say too mockingly. " 'At Christmas a child needs a woman.' "

"I should have taken Janey into my secret," Tim said dryly. "Only she would have felt sorry for Johnny and said this was no place for her on Christmas."

"Maybe she'd have been right," Kate said sharply. "Maybe you'd better take this waif to Janey right now and—"

The doorbell interrupted. "That must be Johnny's puppy," Tim said.

Kate forgot her part of the anger. "A puppy? She could not possibly keep one at the home."

The bell rang again, sharp and impatient. Tim turned. "No," he said, levelly. "But she could keep one here."

Amazement kept Kate silent.

Johnny chose that moment to come down the hall, her arms loaded with awkwardly wrapped packages. She deposited them on the nearest chair and ran to take the puppy in her arms. She didn't go into ecstasies the way some children would have done, but her hands caressed the little dog the way they had the pink comforter—lightly, delicately, lovingly.

The puppy's tongue swiped her cheek. Her eyes were velvet brown come to life. "Will you keep him for me?" she asked Kate. "Will you? And then maybe I could come and visit you sometime and see him."

Again, that crazy lump in Kate's throat. She went quickly into the living room and stood before the fire. That wall about her heart was threatening to crumble, that wall she had built up against hurt and the whole world.

She heard Johnny ask, "Did I say something wrong?"

And Tim's gentle voice. "No, dear, you didn't. Come on, let's fix the tree."

Kate sat in a big, low chair and tried not to watch. The puppy romped on the floor, and the firelight danced on Johnny's absorbed face and tangled in her hair. Tim fixed the colored lights, and Johnny turned them on, then sat back on her heels to admire them.

"Just like a storybook," she said softly. "It is the beautifulest tree there ever was in all the world."

She disappeared and came back a moment later with her hairbrush. She asked Kate shyly, "If I sit on the low stool, will you brush my hair? No one ever did."

Why should words like these sting her eyes with tears? Kate wondered. Her hands were clumsy, and the silky strands of hair clung to her fingers like live things. She braided them carefully and tied the ends with bits of ribbon. She suddenly remembered that she hadn't bought a gift for the child. At least she could have done that much! The child was not to blame for Tim's trick and for the year-long ache in her heart. Johnny curled down on the rug before the fire with the puppy in her arms. She might have been the ghost of Kate's little boy made feminine and come to life. Johnny tipped her head back to look at Tim.

"The puppy doesn't know that I'm ugly, does he? He likes me just the same as if I'm pretty."

Tim looked at her, and then across the room to Kate as if to say, *Take over; I have done all I could.*

"Whoever told you a stupid thing like that?" Kate gasped.

Johnny stared into the fire. Her fingers absently scratched the puppy's ear. "Oh, all the girls at the home," she said calmly. "They say that's why no one ever adopted me. People want pretty children, 'less they are borned to them, and then they don't know the difference, I guess."

Her acceptance of something beyond her control amazed and humbled Kate. For a child as lovely as this to think a thing like that, to have no special corner in all the world for her own . . . Kate failed to remember that once, so short a time ago, she had thought Johnny homely.

She studied the top of the girl's firelit head. "How would you like to be adopted by us?" she asked abruptly. The room seemed to hold its breath, waiting. Kate sensed that the last few days had been a prelude to this moment, to the rebirth of the old Kate, long buried beneath a mound of selfishness. She dared not look at Tim.

"You mean," Johnny said breathlessly, in wonder, "we would be a *family*?"

Kate's voice echoed the wonder. "I mean exactly that," she said softly.

Johnny cried then. Huge tears, boiling over and spilling down her face. "I'd be real good," she said, gulping. "I could help you."

Kate bent over and wiped away the tears. "But now," she said gently, "you need to go to bed. Come along, and I'll tuck you in."

Kate went first to her room and gathered up the comforter, and then came back and spread it on the bed. Tim leaned in the doorway, watching, and she knew with a swift upsurge of happiness that he had seen the miracle of this night. The thread of love was still there, fine and tightly spun, made stronger by the presence of this child.

Johnny climbed between the sheets and smoothed the comforter. "But that is yours," she protested.

"No, it is yours now. From me to you," Kate said. "This is Christmas now, you know."

"That is such a lovely word," Johnny sighed, her eyes already heavy with sleep.

Kate kissed the firm little cheek as she had kissed another small cheek on other nights. "A lovely word," she agreed softly. "Now go to sleep, Johnny Christmas."

At Lowest Ebb

Author Unknown

In 2002, the eleventh Christmas in My Heart *became a reality. One of the stories in the collection really resonated with me, mainly because it brought back memories of my childhood in Latin America. My missionary parents had very little extra money to buy presents with. Our last, best hope centered in the Dorcas barrel that sometimes came from a church in the United States. More often than not, it would be filled with things none of us (including my brother Romayne or my sister Marjorie) had any interest in. Obviously, there were valid reasons why well-used cast-off clothes and toys were tossed in rather than things we might long for. Our parents would always try their best to console us for what had been heaved into the barrel by church parishioners in the United States.*

* * * * *

I remember a day one winter that stands out like a boulder in my life. The weather was unusually cold, our salary had not been regularly paid, and it did not meet our needs when it was.

My husband was away much of the time, traveling from one district to another. Our boys were well, but my little Ruth was ailing, and at best none of us were decently clothed. I patched and repatched, with spirits sinking to the lowest ebb. The water gave out in the well and the wind blew through cracks in the floor.

The people in this frontier parish were kind, and generous too; but the settlement was new, and each family was struggling for itself. Little by little, at the time I needed it most, my faith began to waver.

Early in life I was taught to take God at His word, and I thought my lesson was well learned. I had lived upon the promises in dark times until I knew, as David did, "who was my fortress and deliverer." Now a daily prayer for forgiveness was all that I could offer.

My husband's overcoat was hardly thick enough for October, and he was often obliged to ride miles to attend some meeting or funeral. Many times our breakfast was Indian cake and a cup of tea without sugar.

Christmas was coming; the children always expected their presents. I remember the ice was thick and smooth, and the boys were each craving a pair of skates. Ruth, in some unaccountable way, had taken a fancy that the dolls I had made were no longer suitable. She wanted a nice large one and insisted on praying for it.

I knew it was impossible but, oh! How I wanted to give each child a present. It seemed as if God had deserted us, but I did not tell my husband this. He worked so earnestly and heartily I supposed him to be as hopeful as ever. I kept the sitting room cheerful with an open fire, and I tried to serve our scanty meals as invitingly as I could.

The morning before Christmas James was called to see a sick man. I put up a piece of bread for his lunch (it was the best I could do), wrapped my plaid shawl around his neck, and then tried to whisper a promise as I often had,

but the words died away upon my lips. I let him go without it.

That was a dark, hopeless day. I coaxed the children to bed early, for I could not bear their talk. When Ruth went, I listened to her prayer. She asked for the last time most explicitly for her doll and for skates for her brothers. Her bright face looked so lovely when she whispered to me "You know, I think they'll be here early tomorrow morning, Mama" that I thought I'd be willing to move heaven and earth to save her from disappointment. I sat down alone and gave way to the most bitter tears.

Before long James returned, chilled and exhausted. As he drew off his boots the thin stockings slipped off with them, and his feet were red with cold.

"I wouldn't treat a dog that way, let alone a faithful servant," I said. Then, as I glanced up and saw the hard lines in his face and the look of despair, it flashed across me: James had let go, too.

I brought him a cup of tea, feeling sick and dizzy at the very thought. He took my hand, and we sat for an hour without a word. I wanted to die and meet God and tell Him His promise wasn't true. My soul was so full of rebellious despair.

There came a sound of bells, a quick stop, and a loud knock at the door. James

sprang up to open it. There stood Deacon White. "A box came by express just before dark. I brought it around as soon as I could get away. Reckoned it might be for Christmas. 'At any rate,' I said to myself, 'they shall have it tonight.' There is a turkey my wife asked me to fetch along, and these other things I believe belong to you."

There was a basket of potatoes and a bag of flour. Talking all the time, he carried in the box, and then with a hearty goodnight he rode away.

Still without speaking, James found a chisel and opened the box. He drew out first a thick red blanket, and we saw that beneath was full of clothing. It seemed at that moment as if Christ fastened upon me a look of reproach. James sat down and covered his face with his hands. "I can't touch them!" he exclaimed. "I haven't been true, just when God was trying me to see if I could hold out. Do you think I could not see how you were suffering? And I had no word of comfort to offer. I know now how to preach the awfulness of turning away from God."

"James," I said, clinging to him, "don't take it to heart like this. I am to blame; I ought to have helped you. We will ask Him together to forgive us."

"Wait a moment, dear, I cannot talk now," he said. Then he went into another room.

I knelt down, and my heart broke. In an instant all the darkness, all the stubbornness, rolled away. Jesus came again and stood before me, but with the loving word "Daughter!"

Sweet promises of tenderness and joy flooded my soul. I was so lost in praise and gratitude that I forgot everything else. I don't know how long it was before James came back,

but I knew he too had found peace.

"Now, my dear wife," he said, "let us thank God together." And he then poured out words of praise—Bible words, for nothing else could express our thanksgiving.

It was eleven o'clock, the fire was low, and there was the great box, and nothing touched but the warm blanket we needed. We piled on some fresh logs, lighted two candles, and began to examine our treasures.

We drew out an overcoat—I made James try it on—just the right size. And I danced around him, for all my light-heartedness had returned. Then there was a cloak, and he insisted in seeing me in it. My spirits always infected him, and we both laughed like foolish children.

There was a warm suit of clothes and three pairs of woolen hose. There was a dress for me and yards of flannel, a pair of Arctic overshoes for each of us. In mine was a slip of paper. I have it now and mean to hand it down to my children. On it was written Jacob's blessing to Asher: "Thy shoes shall be iron and brass, and as thy days so shall thy strength be." In the gloves (evidently for James) the same dear hand had written: "I, the Lord thy God, will hold thy right hand, saying unto thee: Fear not, I will help thee."

It was a wonderful box and had been packed with thoughtful care. There was a suit of clothes for each of the boys and a little red gown for Ruth. There were mittens, scarves, and hoods. Down in the center was a box. We opened it—and there was a great wax doll. I burst into tears again. James wept with me for joy. It was too much. And then we both exclaimed again, for close behind it came two pairs of skates. There were books for us to read (some

of them I had yearned for), stories for the children to read, aprons and underclothing, knots of ribbon, a gay little tidy, a lovely photograph, needles, buttons, and thread, a muff, and an envelope containing a ten-dollar gold piece.

At last we cried over everything we took up. It was past midnight, and we were faint and exhausted with happiness. I made a cup of tea, cut a fresh loaf of bread, and James boiled some eggs. We drew up the table before the fire, and how we enjoyed our supper! And then we sat, talking over our life, and how sure a help God had always proved.

You should have seen the children the next morning! The boys raised a shout at the sight of their skates. Ruth caught up her doll and hugged it tightly without a word. Then she went into her room and knelt by her bed.

When she came back she whispered to me, "I knew it would be here, Mama, but I wanted to thank God just the same, you know."

My husband then said, "Look here, wife, see the difference?"

We went to the window, and there were the boys out of the house already, skating on the ice with all their might.

My husband and I both tried to return thanks to the church in the East that had sent us the box and have tried to return thanks unto God every day since. Hard times have come again and again, but we have trusted in Him, dreading nothing so much as to doubt His protecting care. Again and again, we have proved that "they that seek the Lord shall not want of any good thing."

Van Valkenberg's Christmas Gift

Elizabeth G. Jordan

I can never pick up a copy of our twelfth collection (2003) without thinking of Dr. James Dobson of Focus on the Family and his love of heart-tugging Christmas stories. During one of my visits to Focus on the Family in Colorado Springs, he idly remarked to his large staff, "Joe Wheeler—America's Keeper of the Story." Only days later, I was told that Dr. Dobson wanted me to know that I was free to use that quotation in our future books. I dedicated Christmas in My Heart *12 to him, and he was almost overwhelmed by it. He is a kindred spirit in that we both love stories that deeply move us.*

One of the stories in book 12 is titled "Van Valkenberg's Christmas Gift," written by Elizabeth G. Jordan. It features an unusual plot (one of a kind) in our series. I have searched but have been unable to find its publishing roots. I believe you will be as unable to forget this story as I have been.

* * * * *

The *Chicago Limited* was pulling out of the Grand Central Station in New York as Dr. Henry Van Valkenberg submitted his ticket to the gateman. He dashed through, pushing the indignant official to one side, and made a leap for the railing of the last car of the train. It was wet and slippery and maddeningly elusive, but he caught it, and clung to it valiantly, his legs actively seeking a resting place on the snow-covered steps of the platform. Even as he hung there, offering to his fellow travelers this inspiring illustration of athletic prowess and the strenuous life, he was painfully conscious that the position was not a dignified one for a stout gentleman of sixty who held an exalted position in the scientific world. He pictured to himself the happy smiles of those who were looking on, and he realized that his conception of their hearty enjoyment had not been exaggerated when he glanced back at them after a friendly brakeman had dragged him on board.

Dr. Van Valkenberg smiled a little ruefully as he thanked the man and rubbed the aching surface of his hand, which not even his thick kid gloves had protected. Then he pulled himself together, picked up the books and newspapers he had dropped and which the bystanders had enthusiastically hurled after him, and sought his haven in the sleeping car. When he reached his section, he stood for a moment with his back to the passengers to put some of his belongings in the rack above his head. As he was trying to arrange them properly he heard a voice behind him.

"O-oh! Were you hurt?" it said. "I was so 'fraid you were going to fall."

Dr. Van Valkenberg, who was a tall man, turned and looked down from his great height. At his feet stood a baby; at least she seemed a baby to him, although she was very dignified and wholly self-possessed and fully four years old. She was looking up at him with dark brown eyes, which wore an absurdly anxious expression. In that instant of quick observation he noticed that her wraps had been removed and that she wore a white dress and had yellow curls, among which, on one side of her head, a small black bow lay somberly.

She was so delightful in her almost maternal solicitude that he smiled irrepressibly, though he answered with the ceremoniousness she seemed to expect.

"Why, no, thank you," he said. "I am not hurt. Didn't you see the kind man help me onto the car?"

There was a subdivided titter from the other passengers over this touching admission of helplessness, but the human atom below drew a long, audible sigh of relief.

"I'm very glad," she said, with dignity. "I was 'fraid he hurt you." She turned as she spoke and toddled into the section opposite his, where a plain but kindly faced elderly woman was sitting. She lifted her charge to the seat beside her, and the child rose to her knees, pressed her pink face against the windowpane, and looked out at the snow that was falling heavily.

Dr. Van Valkenberg settled back in his seat and tried to read his newspaper, but for some reason the slight incident in which he and the little girl had figured moved him strangely. It had been a long time since anyone had looked at him like that! He was not a person who aroused sympathy. He conscientiously endeavored to follow the newspaper's report on the president's latest oracular utterances on the trust problem, but his eyes turned often to the curly head at the window opposite. They were well-trained, observant eyes, and they read the woman as not the mother but a paid attendant—a trained nurse, probably, with fifteen years of admirable, cold, scientific service behind her.

Why was she with the child? he wondered.

It was Christmas Eve—not the time for a baby girl to be traveling. Then his glance fell again on the black bow among the yellow curls and on the white dress with its black shoulder-knots,* and the explanation came to him.

An orphan, of course, on her way West to a new home, in charge of the matter-of-fact nurse who was dozing comfortably in the corner of her seat. To whom was she going? Perhaps to grandparents, where she would be spoiled and wholly happy; or quite possibly to more distant relatives, where she might find a grudging welcome. Dear little embryo woman, with her sympathetic heart already attuned to the world's gamut of pain. She should have been dancing under a Christmas tree, or hanging up her tiny stocking in the warm chimney corner of some cozy nursery. The heart of the man swelled at the thought, and he recognized the sensation with a feeling of surprised annoyance. What was all this to him—to an old bachelor who knew nothing of children except their infantile ailments, and who had supposed that he cared for them as little as he understood them?

Still, it was Christmas. His mind swung back to that. He himself had rebelled at the unwelcome prospect of Christmas Eve and Christmas Day in a sleeping car—he, without even nephews and nieces to lighten the gloom of his lonely house. The warm human sympathy of the man and the sweet traditions of his youth rose in protest against the spectacle of a lonely child, traveling through the night

---

* In earlier times, surviving family members wore black for an extended period of time after the death of a close family member.

toward some distant home which she had never seen, and where coldness—even neglect—might await her. Then he reminded himself that this was all imagination, and that he might be wholly wrong in his theory of the journey, and he called himself a fool for his pains. Still, the teasing interest and an elusive but equally teasing memory held his thoughts.

Darkness was falling, but the porter had not begun to light the lamps, and heavy shadows were rising from the corners of the car. Dr. Van Valkenberg's little neighbor turned from the gloom without to the gloom within and made an impulsive movement toward the drowsy woman opposite her. The nurse did not stir, and the little girl sat silent, her brown eyes shining in the half-light and her dimpled hands folded in her lap. The physician leaned across the aisle.

"Won't you come over and visit me?" he asked. "I am very lonely, and I have no one to take care of me."

She slid off the seat at once, with great alacrity. "I'd like to," she said, "but I must ask Nana. I must always ask Nana now," she added, with dutiful emphasis, " 'fore I do anything."

* * * * *

She laid her hand on the gloved fingers of the nurse as she spoke, and the woman opened her eyes, shot a quick glance at the man, and nodded. She had not been asleep. Dr. Van Valkenberg rose and lifted his visitor to the seat beside him, where her short legs stuck out in uncompromising rigidity, and her tiny hands returned demurely to their former position in her lap. She took up the conversation where it had been interrupted.

"I can take care of you," she said brightly. "I taked care of Mama a great deal, and I gave her her med'cin'."

He replied by placing a cushion behind her back and forming a resting place for her feet by building an imposing pyramid, of which his suitcase was the base. Then he turned to her with the smile women loved.

"Very well," he said. "If you really are going to take care of me I must know your name. You see," he explained, "I might need you in the night to get me a glass of water or something. Just think how disappointing it would be if I should call you by the wrong name and some other little girl came!"

She laughed. "You say funny things," she said, contentedly. "But there isn't any other little girl in the car. I looked soon as I came on, 'cos I wanted one to play with. I like little girls. I like little boys too," she added, with innocent expansiveness.

"Then we'll play I'm a little boy. You'd never believe it, but I used to be. You haven't told me your name," he reminded her.

"Hope," she said, promptly. "Do you think it is a nice name?" She made the inquiry with an anxious interest that seemed to promise immediate change if the name displeased him.

He reassured her. "I think Hope is the nicest name a little girl could have, except one," he said. "The nicest little girl I ever knew was named Katharine. She grew to be a nice big girl, too—and has little girls of her own now, no doubt," he added, half to himself.

"Were you a little boy when she was a little girl?" asked his visitor with flattering interest.

"Oh, no; I was a big man, just as I am now. Her father was my friend, and she lived in a white house with an old garden where there were all kinds of flowers. She used to play there when she was a tiny baby, just big enough to crawl along the paths. Later, she learned to walk there, and then the gardener had to follow her to see that she didn't pick *all* the flowers. I used to carry her around and hold her high up so she could pull the apples and pears off the trees. When she grew larger, I gave her a horse and taught her to ride. She seemed like my very own little girl. But by and by she grew up and became a young lady, and, well, she went away from me, and I never had another little girl."

He had begun the story to interest the child. He found, as he went on, that it still interested him.

"Did she go to heaven?" asked the little girl softly.

"Oh, dear, no," answered the doctor, with brisk cheerfulness.

"Then why didn't she keep on being your little girl always?" was the next leading question.

The doctor hesitated a moment. He was making the discovery that after many years old wounds can reopen and throb. No one had ever been brave enough to broach to him the subject of this single love affair that he was now discussing, he told himself, like a garrulous old woman. He was anxious to direct the conversation into other channels, but there was a certain compelling demand in the brown eyes upturned to his.

"Well, you see," he explained, "other boys liked her too. And when she became a young lady, other men liked her. So, finally—one of them took her away from me." He uttered the last words wearily, and the sensitive atom at his side seemed to understand why. Her little hand slipped into his.

"Why didn't you ask her to please stay with you?" she persisted, pityingly.

"I did," he told her. "But you see, she liked the other man better."

"Oh-h-h." The word came out long-drawn and breathless. "I don't see how she possedly could!"

There was such sorrow for the victim and scorn for the offender in the tone that, combined with the none-too-subtle compliment, it was too much for Dr. Van Valkenberg's self-control. He threw back his gray head and burst into an almost boyish shout of laughter, which effectually cleaned the atmosphere of sentimental memories. He suddenly realized, too, that he had not been giving the child the cheerful holiday evening he had intended.

"Where are you going to hang up your stockings tonight?" he asked.

A shade fell over her sensitive face. "I can't hang them up," she answered, soberly. "Santa Claus doesn't travel on trains, Nana says. But p'r'aps he'll have something waiting for me when I get to Cousin Gertie's," she added, with sweet hopefulness.

"Nana is always right," said the doctor solemnly, "and of course you must do exactly as she says. But I heard that Santa Claus was going to get on the train tonight at Buffalo; and I believe," he added slowly and impressively, "that if he found a pair of small black stockings hanging from that section he'd fill them!"

Her eyes sparkled.

"Then I'll ask Nana," she said. "An' if she says I may hang them, I will. But one," she added, conscientiously, "has a teeny, weeny hole in the toe. Do you think he would mind that?"

He reassured her on this point and turned to the nurse, who was now wide awake and absorbed in a novel. The car was brilliantly lighted, and the passengers were beginning to respond to the first dinner call.

"I beg your pardon," he said. "I've taken a great fancy to your little charge, and I want your help to carry out a plan of mine. I have suggested to Hope that she hang up her stockings tonight. I have every reason to believe that Santa Claus will get on this train at Buffalo. In fact," he added, smiling, "I mean to telegraph him."

The nurse hesitated a moment. He drew his card case from his pocket and handed her one of the bits of paste-board it contained.

"I have no evil designs," he added, cheerfully. "If you are a New Yorker you may possibly know who I am."

The woman's face lit up as she read the name. She turned toward him impulsively, with a very pleasant smile. "Indeed I do, Doctor," she said. "Who does not? Dr. Abbey sent for you last week," she added, "for a consultation over the last case I had—this child's mother. But you were out of town. We were all so disappointed. It seems strange that we should meet now."

"Patient died?" asked the physician, with professional brevity.

"Yes, doctor."

He rose from his seat.

"Now that you have my credentials," he added, cordially, "I want you and Hope to dine with me. You will, won't you?"

The upholstered cheerfulness of the dining car found favor in the sight of Hope. She conducted herself, however, with her usual dignity, broken only occasionally by an ecstatic wriggle as the prospective visit of Santa Claus crossed her mind. Her dinner, superintended by an eminent physician and a trained nurse, was naturally a simple and severely hygienic one, but here, too, her admirable training was evident. She ate cheerfully her bowl of bread and milk and wasted no longing glances on the plum pudding.

* * * * *

Later, in the feverish excitement of hanging up her stockings, going to bed, and peeping through the curtains to catch Santa Claus, a little of her extraordinary repose of manner deserted her. But she fell asleep at last, with great reluctance.

When the curtains round her berth had ceased trembling, a most unusual procession wended its silent way toward Dr. Van Valkenberg's section. In some secret manner the news had gone from one end to the other of the "Special" that a little girl in section nine, car *Floradora*, had hung up her stockings for Santa Claus. The hearts of fathers, mothers, and doting uncles responded at once. Suitcases were unlocked, great trunks were opened, mysterious bundles were unwrapped, and from all these sources came gifts of surprising fitness. Small daughters and nieces,

sleeping in Western cities, might well have turned restlessly in their beds had they seen the presents designed for them drop into a pair of tiny stockings and pile up on the floor below.

A succession of long-drawn, ecstatic breaths and happy gurgles awoke the passengers on car *Floradora* at an unseemly hour Christmas morning, and a small white figure, clad informally in a single garment, danced up and down the aisle, dragging carts and woolly lambs behind it. Occasionally there was the squeak of a talking doll, and always there was the patter of small feet and the soft cooing of a child's voice, punctuated by the exquisite music of a child's laughter. Dawn was just approaching, and the lamps, still burning, flared pale in the gray light. But in the length of that car there was no soul so base as to long for silence and the pillow. Crabbed old faces looked out between the curtains and smiled; eyes long unused to tears felt a sudden strange moisture.

Dr. Van Valkenberg had risen almost as early as Hope, and possibly the immaculate freshness of his attire contrasted with the scantiness of her own induced that young lady to retire from observation for a short time and emerge clothed for general society. Even during this brief retreat in the dressing room the passengers heard her breathless voice, high-pitched in her excitement, chattering incessantly to the responsive Nana.

Throughout the day the snow still fell, and the outside world seemed far away and dreamlike to Dr. Van Valkenberg. The real things were this train, cutting its way through the snow, and this little child, growing deeper into his heart with each moment that passed. The situation was

unique but easy enough to understand, he told himself. He had merely gone back twenty-five years to that other child whom he had cherished in infancy and loved and lost in womanhood. He had been very lonely, how lonely he had only recently begun to realize, and he was becoming an old man whose life lay behind him. He crossed the aisle suddenly and sat down beside the nurse, leaving Hope singing her doll to sleep in his section. There was something almost diffident in his manner as he spoke.

"Will you tell me all you know about the child?" he asked. "She interests me greatly and appeals to me very strongly, probably because she's so much like someone I used to know."

The nurse closed her book and looked at him curiously. She had heard much of him, but nothing that would explain this interest in a strange child. He himself could not have explained it. He knew only that he felt it, powerfully and compellingly.

"Her name is Hope Armitage," she said quietly. "Her mother, who has just died, was a widow—Mrs. Katharine Armitage. They were poor, and Mrs. Armitage seemed to have no relatives. She had saved a little, enough to pay most of her expenses at the hospital, and—" She hesitated a moment, and then went on. "I am telling you everything very frankly because you are you, but it was done quietly enough. We all loved the woman. She was very unusual and patient and charming. All the nurses who had had anything to do with her cried when she died. We felt that she might have been saved if she had come to us in time, but she was worked out. She had earned her living by sewing after her husband's death three years ago, and

she kept at it day and night. She hadn't much constitution to begin with, and none when she came to us. She was so sweet, so brave, yet so desperately miserable over leaving her little girl alone in the world—"

Dr. Van Valkenberg sat silent. It was true, then. This was Katharine's child. Had he not known it? Could he have failed to know it, whenever or wherever they had met? He had not known of the death of Armitage nor of the subsequent poverty of his widow, but he had known Katharine's baby, he now told himself, the moment he saw her.

"Well," the nurse resumed, "after she died we raised a small fund to buy some clothes for Hope and to take her to Chicago to her new home. Mrs. Armitage has a cousin there who has agreed to take her in. None of the relatives came to the funeral; there are not many of them, and the Chicago people haven't much money, I fancy. They offered to send Hope's fare, or even to come for her, if it was absolutely necessary; but they seemed very much relieved when we wrote that I would bring her out."

Dr. Van Valkenberg did not speak at once. He was hardly surprised. Life was full of extraordinary situations, and his profession had brought him face-to-face with many of them. Nevertheless, a deep solemnity filled him and a strange peace settled over him. He turned to the nurse with something of this in his face and voice.

"I want her," he said, briefly. "Her mother and father were old friends of mine, and this thing looks like fate. Will they give her to me—these Chicago people—do you think?"

Tears filled the woman's eyes. "Indeed they will," she said, "and gladly. There was"—she hesitated—"there was even some talk of sending her to an institution before they finally decided to take her. Dear little Hope—how happy she will be with you!"

He left her and went back to the seat where Hope sat, crooning to the doll. Sitting down, he gathered them both up in his arms and a thrill shot through him as he looked at the yellow curls resting against his breast. Her child—her little helpless baby—now his child, to love and care for. He was not a religious man; nevertheless, a prayer rose spontaneously in his heart. But there was a plea to be made—a second plea, somewhat like the one he had made the mother. This time he felt that he knew the answer.

"Hope," he said, gently, "once, long ago, I asked a little girl to come and live with me, and she would not come. Now I want to ask you to come and stay with me always and be my own little girl, and let me take care of you and make you happy. Will you come?"

* * * * *

The radiance of June sunshine broke out upon her face and shone in the brown eyes upturned to his. How well he knew that look! Hope did not turn toward Nana, and that significant omission touched him deeply. She seemed to feel that here was a question she alone must decide. She drew a long breath as she looked up at him.

"Really, truly?" she asked. Then, as he nodded without speaking, she saw something in his face that was new to her. It was nothing to frighten a little girl, for it was very sweet and tender; but for one second she thought her new friend was going to cry! She put both arms around his neck

and replied softly, with the exquisite maternal cadences her voice had taken on in her first words to him when he entered the car. "I'll be your own little girl, and I'll take care of you too. You know, you said I could."

Dr. Van Valkenberg turned to the nurse. "I shall go with you to her cousin's from the train," he announced. "I'm ready to give them all the proofs they need that I'm a suitable guardian for the child. But," he added, with a touch of the boyishness that had never left him, "I want this matter settled now."

The long train pounded its way into the station at Chicago, and the nurse hurriedly put on Hope's coat and gloves and fastened the ribbons of her hood under her chin. Dr. Van Valkenberg summoned a porter.

"Take care of all these things," he said, indicating both sets of possessions with a sweep of the arm. "I shall have my hands full with my little daughter."

He gathered her into his arms as he spoke, and she nestled against his broad chest with a child's unconscious satisfaction in the strength and firmness of his clasp. The lights of the great station were twinkling in the early dusk as he stepped off the train, and the place was noisy with the greetings exchanged between the passengers and their waiting friends.

"Merry Christmas!" "Merry Christmas!" sounded on every side. Everybody was absorbed and excited, yet there were few who did not find time to turn a last look on a singularly attractive little child, held above the crowd in the arms of a tall man. She was laughing triumphantly as he bore her through the throng, and his heart was in his eyes as he smiled back at her.

Elizabeth G. Jordan (1867–1947), of Milwaukee, Wisconsin, was prominent early in the twentieth century as a critic, short story writer, novelist, and playwright. She was a literary advisor to Harper & Brothers and a drama critic for America.

A White Christmas

Author Unknown

Another Christmas season neared, and with it, our thirteenth anthology of Christmas stories was published in late summer 2004.

Of the twenty-one stories in the thirteenth collection, I have selected "White Christmas," which is little known—except for a popular song that features some of the same lines. I have not been able to discover who wrote it.

* * * * *

The train was crowded, and the only seat left was beside a young boy who looked to be no more than fifteen years of age. The minister set his handbag down and sat down beside the boy. Desiring to be pleasant, he made some commonplace remark about the fact that everyone was hurrying home for Christmas; but the boy didn't answer—he had been crying. Puzzled, the minister ceased his attempt at conversation and waited for the boy to speak.

Turning away from him, the minister gazed out the opposite window at the snow-covered landscape. It was going to be a white Christmas, all right. Great flakes were coming down, and the window was almost covered. He thought of the long ride ahead of him and wondered how far the boy had to go. *Too bad the boy is in trouble,* he thought to himself. It didn't seem right for a boy to cry on Christmas Eve.

As if sensing the preacher's thoughts, the boy began to wipe his eyes. When he finally looked around, he was trying to act as if nothing were wrong. The minister smiled at him, and he answered with a tremulous grin that wobbled a bit around the edges.

"It surely looks cold out there," the boy volunteered.

Grasping at the chance to talk, the preacher began to tell him of the cold days he had seen during his boyhood, of the trying job of milking two cows in subzero weather, and of the pleasure of a roaring fire in the living room at night after the chores were through.

"You know, I sometimes think we can stand almost anything if we have something nice to look forward to. Take me, for instance. I've been traveling for a long time, and I have a good long trip ahead of me yet; but I know that when I do get home my family will be waiting for me, and my little boy will be looking forward to his Christmas presents. It's a great thing, going home for Christmas."

The minister watched the boy and saw a quiver pass over the sensitive young face as he choked back a sob, and then answered, "It is—sometimes."

Clumsy remark! said the preacher to himself. *Now you've ventured in where you shouldn't. Perhaps the boy has recently lost his mother or father.* Then aloud he said, "Excuse me, son; maybe I said the wrong thing. I don't know about your troubles, and you don't have to tell me—unless

you want to—but I'm a preacher, and I might be able to help you with your problem."

The boy looked at the minister for a moment, and then said, "I want to tell you—I've got to tell someone!"

"All right; then let's hear it."

The boy laid his head back and looked out the window as he began. "I guess I don't deserve much Christmas, but I can't help wanting one. I've been away from home four months now. I became discouraged with school and all the chores I had to do. Nothing enjoyable ever seemed to happen in our town. Father has a store, and he farms on the side. Our place is just on the edge of town. We keep cows too. I got tired of milking them in the winter mornings before daylight and then coming home from school to feed and water and milk them all over again. All of the older boys were getting jobs.

"One day I ran away from home. I didn't think much about how bad it was, or how I'd get along after I got to where I was going. I just went. I got on a freight train that went through town early in the morning, and by night I was in Saint Louis. I had never seen a place so big as that, and I was scared. I had some money with me, but it didn't last long. I suppose grown folk can tell how old a boy is, no matter how big he looks. They told me to go back home— but see, that was the trouble. I felt that my parents would be displeased with me; and even if they weren't, I dreaded to go sneaking back like a whipped dog. I was terribly lonesome, especially at night. I went home with another boy, but it wasn't like my home.

"Finally I wrote Father. I didn't give him any address, but I told him I'd be on this train today. If they wanted me, I'd stop; if they didn't want me, I'd keep on going. I suppose it was a foolish thing to do, but I just couldn't stand

it to think of getting a letter from him telling me he didn't want me back, and I didn't want him to come after me. I figured out this way so that it would be easier on all of us. But now I'm scared!"

The preacher looked at his young companion and knew that he meant it. "What are you afraid of, son?" he asked.

"I'm afraid they won't want me."

"But how will you know?"

He rubbed his fist on the steamy windowpane until a small portion was clear. It was growing dark now, and the snow was falling fast, but the few houses stood out as if etched against the soft, fuzzy sky. "Just a little farther," he said in a low voice, and then he hid his eyes. "I can't look," he said desperately. "I can't."

"What is it you're looking for—some sign to let you know whether they're expecting you?"

"Yes, that's it," came the muffled reply. "I told Father that if he wanted me back, tie a white rag to a branch of the old apple tree in the front yard. It is near the railroad, and we can see it plainly. We're almost there now . . . But I can't look!"

He was crying now; the minister's eyes were also misty. Leaning over, he put an arm around the boy and patted his shoulder. "That's all right, son; you don't have to look. I'll be your eyes—I'll tell you when I see it."

"But I'm afraid you won't see it," he sobbed. "I'm afraid they won't tie the rag there; I'm afraid they don't want me anymore."

Suddenly the hoarse note of the train's whistle broke in upon them, and the boy sat up. "We're almost there!" he cried. "You look and see—I can't."

The train was slowing to a stop as it came around a long curve. The minister strained his eyes to peer through the falling snow—he must not fail. But he need not have worried, for a half-blind man could have seen that tree.

Laughing and crying, the minister pulled the boy up to the window. "Look there!" he said. "The apple tree is all bloomed out!"

And indeed it was, for upon its bare branches hung not one but at least fifty white rags that gaily fluttered in the brisk wind, like victory banners of forgiving love.